CRAZY KILL RANGE

By the same author

TIM'S MOUNTAIN

THE SILVER HILLS

MISTER JIM

MOUNTAIN MAN

BEAVER WATER

AMIKUK

ILLUSTRATED BY *Lorence Bjorklund*

CRAZY KILL RANGE

Rutherford G. Montgomery

THE WORLD PUBLISHING COMPANY

CLEVELAND AND NEW YORK

Published by The World Publishing Company
2231 West 110th Street, Cleveland 2, Ohio

Published simultaneously in Canada by
Nelson, Foster & Scott Ltd.

Library of Congress Catalog Card Number: 63–10860

First Edition

1 2 3 4 5 67 66 65 64 63

For the Nutall clan:
Stuart, Scott and Stan

Contents

A Place to Hide

THE SUN was high over the Crazy Kill Mountains. It penetrated the depths of Shadow Canyon, and its rays were reflected from the foaming waters of Crazy River. The voice of the river rose up to wooded benches overshadowed by ridges which stood naked above the timber line. This was high country, wild and remote, a haven for bears, wolves, cougars, and wild horses.

Below, where the canyon opened into a valley, there were larger meadows and less timber. These meadows furnished horse pasture for Major Howard's Boiling Springs Ranch, whose stock carried the Bar T brand. The major raised white-faced cattle, but his main interest was fine horses which

9

he bred for showing and racing. His big house in the valley was crowded with trophies he had won. He scorned the practices of Eastern stables. His mares ran loose in a big, tightly fenced pasture under the protection of a big black stallion called Midnight.

The spring sun beat down upon the pasture. Midnight stood on high ground watching over his herd. He had once been a wild stallion and he had never forgotten the things he had learned. He still refused to allow any of his twenty mares to wander away from the grazing herd. Stray mares invited attack from prowling cougars or renegade bears. The stout aspen poles of the pasture fence prevented Midnight from driving his herd up into the wild country above, which always seemed to beckon him.

Black Lady stood at the upper edge of the herd. She was a fine black mare from a long line of racing horses. She shook her head restlessly as she looked up toward the forested benches above the pasture. Major Howard had cleared all the underbrush off the slope to make room for grass. There was no thicket cover and this worried Black Lady.

The other mares were grazing or sunning themselves; several lay drowsing on the grass. Midnight stood staring up at the mountains. Black Lady moved cautiously toward the fence, keeping an eye on the stallion. She was filled with an age-old urge to be alone. Very soon her foal would be born, and instinct told her to find a secluded spot where the foal could have a few undisturbed days in which to get strength into its legs, a place where no harm would come to it. She started walking alongside of the fence.

She passed a stand of young spruce that hid her from the watchful eyes of the stallion. After advancing a few yards she halted. There had been a tall pine in the grove; now it lay across the fence, its white heart split open by a bolt of lightning. The ancient pine had fallen during a thunderstorm the night before. Its wounds were so fresh that sticky beads of resin sap glistened in the sun. Its heavy trunk had flattened the fence.

Black Lady looked back, then stepped over the smashed rails. Her head came up as she loped toward a wall of scrub oak bordering a forest of pine and spruce. Midnight could not see her because she kept the spruce grove between herself and the pasture. Within minutes she had swerved into a narrow opening in the scrub oak.

As she entered the timber a crested jay started screaming loudly. Another jay added its voice. Black Lady increased her pace to a gallop. The screaming of the jays—forest sentinels who warn of the approach of prowlers—would certainly alert Midnight. The big stallion would investigate.

Midnight's angry scream rang up through the

timber, sending her forward in a panic. She swung past a small clearing which gave her a brief view of the pasture below. Midnight had charged up the pasture, but he was moving away from the break in the fence.

Black Lady kept on moving, slowed now to a trot. The gloom of the dense forest did not suit her needs. She wanted shade, but she also wanted a little open park with grass and a small stream for water. No grass grew under the pines and spruce.

She came to the rim of Shadow Canyon following a deer trail, and descended. The brief midday sun no longer reached the bottom of the canyon. The air was damp and gloomy. This was no place for a foal to be born. She moved on over the rock-strewn canyon floor until she came to a steep trail which angled upward. The compelling urgency inside her made her climb as fast as she could. Without planning, she was making sure that none of the major's range riders would be able to trail her. The rocky ground left no prints.

She stopped twice to catch her breath before she reached the rim above. She came out on the north rim which put her in the wild country above Shadow Canyon. Here the benches looked like the country she was seeking. She trotted across a small park and climbed a ridge. From its elevation she saw a small stream foaming down to a notch in the canyon rim where it plunged downward in a mist of spray, tumbling toward Crazy River.

She was thirsty after her hard climb, and a feeling of hunger had begun to stir inside her. She trotted down to the stream and drank deeply, then turned away from the creek and started pulling grass. After grazing for a half hour she moved on up along the stream. Here was a secluded place with many inviting thickets. The only sound that came to her was the hum of insects and the murmur of the creek.

Black Lady had all of the instincts of a horse, but the ways of the wild were unknown to her. She had always depended upon the protection of man, so the alert sixth sense of a wild animal was dormant in her. The only touch of the wild she had ever known came to her through her association with Midnight. She was not aware that an old tom cougar lay on a ledge watching her, his intent yellow eyes following every move she made. When she moved to the edge of a larger bench he slid from the ledge and padded silently along just above her, keeping his tawny form hidden by berry bushes and sage clumps.

On the bench a dozen wild mares were feeding just inside the cover of an aspen grove. Most of them were lean tough mares with little to recommend them except speed and a savage determination to stay alive. The herd had once numbered twenty, but the slower, more dull-witted members had fallen prey to cougars, wolves, or the rifles of range riders. The rifles had taken the biggest toll. Against cougars, wolves or a savage old bear, their leader, Big Baldy, was able to defend them most of the time. He had less luck coping with the rifles of Major Howard's men. All cattlemen hated wild horses because the scrub stallions stole ranch mares.

Big Baldy stood close to the mares at a spot from which he could look out and watch the slopes and the bench. He was a scarred veteran who had earned a reputation for smartness and daring. The three branded mares in his herd bore testimony of his daring. They were fine animals stolen from ranch herds. Two of them had scrub colts at their sides. Big Baldy was restless. He shook his massive square head and pawed the ground. A dozen mares would have satisfied a lesser stallion, but that number did not satisfy the big gray. When darkness settled he would move down country toward the ranches.

If Big Baldy had been born in a pasture under the eyes of men who knew horses, he might have won laurels as a jumper. He had the build for jumping and a natural instinct for it. Few barriers were too high for him to clear. He was disdainful of rail fences, leaping over them when they blocked his path. And he forced his mares to jump, unmindful of disasters which resulted to some of them. Twice he had led them out of corral traps.

Down at the lower end of the bench Black Lady had halted to rest in the shade of a big aspen tree. She was unaware of Big Baldy and his herd. She stood drowsing, her head lowered, her back to a ledge rising from a tangle of cherry and mountain laurel. Laurel branches swayed and jerked close to the base of the ledge. There was a flash of color and a lank form leaped to the ledge and flattened itself there, the yellow body blending with the rock formation. Crouching, belly to the rock, the cougar set himself for a leap which would land him upon the mare's back with smashing force.

Up in the aspen grove the big wide-set eyes of the gray stallion checked the bench and the slopes above and below. They missed nothing that moved. Movement might indicate the approach of danger. But Black Lady didn't move, so he did not spot her.

Black Lady was startled out of her drowsiness by the savage scream of a stallion. She recognized that angry call. Midnight had taught her to react fast when he screamed. She jerked up her head and whirled. An instant later a smashing blow struck her hips, and she felt searing pain as long claws ripped at her back. She staggered but was able to lunge. The big cougar landed on the ground beside her. He reared up and lashed at her, missing by inches. But he did not leap again. He had heard the

scream of the stallion and knew he dared not press
the attack.

Big Baldy had seen the flash of tawny fur as the
cougar left the ledge. He had warned his mares before charging down the slope. They instantly faded
deeper into the grove where they stood watching
him.

Black Lady leaped away from the cougar and
started running up the slope. She whirled when Big
Baldy burst out of the timber. She wanted to get
away from the cougar, but she did not want to have
anything to do with a stallion. She wanted to escape to a place where she could be alone. She broke
for a distant stand of timber in a flash of speed.

If she had not been carrying a colt, she would
have outrun Big Baldy, who abandoned the cougar
when he saw her. As it was he overtook her before
she reached cover. Plunging along beside her he
reached out with bared teeth, ripping at her shoulder, forcing her to change her course. She lashed
back at him with her heels, but he was too powerful
for her. He smashed against her and sent her staggering toward the herd. Every time she tried to bolt
left or right he blocked her. She fled into the timber
and joined the herd, which had now bunched together. As soon as she joined the other mares Big
Baldy stopped lashing at her, and circled to higher

ground where he halted and stood watching the black mare he had captured.

Black Lady had no intention of staying with Big Baldy's herd; even fear of the cougar would not make her stay. But she was badly battered and shaken so she stood watching the big gray, ready to bolt for freedom if he moved far enough away so that she would have a chance to escape. For a while he stood with head up, alert and watchful. He knew what to expect from a newly captured ranch mare. After a half hour he dropped his head and started grazing, moving slowly to higher ground away from the mares.

When the stallion was well up the slope Black Lady made her bid for escape. She darted out of the herd, breaking into the open below the mares, fleeing toward dense timber. Big Baldy screamed once as he thundered after her. She was a prize, and he didn't intend losing her. Black Lady made a good try, but again he caught up with her and turned her back toward the herd. He showed no mercy, and when she halted among the mares her shoulder and rump were bloody from his teeth, and welts had started to form.

The effort Black Lady had put forth sapped her strength. She was in no condition for such strenuous efforts. For months she had grazed peacefully, putting on fat, letting her leg muscles and her body grow soft. She stood trembling, her head down, her flanks heaving as she regained her breath. She was beaten and she knew it. Big Baldy seemed satisfied; he moved off and started pulling grass.

The noisy chattering of a jay aroused Big Baldy. The jay was joined at once by the angry chattering of a chicaree squirrel. The sounds came from a low ridge. Big Baldy moved on his herd menacingly. They crowded together and moved deeper into the grove where they stood waiting his command to stampede. Big Baldy did not give the signal. He moved a little distance down the slope and stood watching the ridge.

He did not have to wait long. Two riders appeared on the ridge moving slowly upward. They were two of Major Howard's men out looking for Black Lady. Big Baldy watched them as they moved along the ridge, ready instantly to stampede his mares if one of them coughed or whinnied, betraying the presence of the herd. He stood there long after the men had disappeared, before returning to the mares.

The black mare had secluded herself in a thicket, but Big Baldy did not bother her. She was not likely to try to escape again. A few lessons soon taught a mare the rules by which a wild herd lived.

Night was approaching, but capturing the black mare had taken the edge off Big Baldy's desire to move on. He decided to let the mares feed in the open during the night.

An owl in the branches above Black Lady hooted mournfully. From a distant ridge came the mating call of a pair of coyotes. Black Lady stirred restlessly and once she nickered softly.

Before midnight a black colt lay beside Black Lady. He kicked his slender legs when she nuzzled him and nickered to him. Soon, he began struggling to get his slender legs under him. After several attempts he got to his feet. The son of Midnight was a husky fellow. By the time the herd moved back to cover for the day he would be able to bounce at his mother's side. At the moment the thing he wanted was milk. He thrust his pink muzzle under Black Lady's flank and drank hungrily.

Black Lady again began thinking of escape, but waited. The colt was too unsteady to do any running. She would have to bide her time. But now that he was born she wanted to get back to familiar pastures.

The colt was as black as his father and he had the same white star in his forehead. His legs indicated that he would be a runner like his mother, but he had his father's chest muscles and heavy bone structure. Major Howard would have marked him as the best prospect to come out of his herd of fine mares.

Dim Trails

THERE WAS one horse who was always close to Big
Baldy's herd but never joined it. Charlie was a gelding who had taken to the wild life by choice. In his
prime he had won races from the best track horses.
He still had speed and staying power. Big Baldy
hated male horses, especially geldings, so Charlie
dared not mingle with the herd. But he could outrun the gray stallion, so that as long as he kept his
wits about him, he was never in danger of being
smashed to pulp. He had forsaken the home pastures
of the Lazy Y when he was turned out to live a life of
retirement, but he had never gotten used to being a
loner; he needed other horses to make him feel
right. He was very much interested in Black Lady

22

and her son. He seemed to know that she was not a wild horse, but a mare who had lived on a ranch and worked for men. He made it his habit always to keep the mare and her black colt in sight.

Ebony was a natural name for the colt, though his mother would not have thought about his color. Nor did she think about his being almost the picture of his father, even to the white star and the white stocking on his left hind foot. Ebony got acquainted with Charlie when he was only a week old. Black Lady was grazing a little apart from the herd and Ebony was playing about in the tall grass, kicking up his heels, shying at rocks and thrusting his muzzle into any bush he came to. He shied around a big boulder and found himself face to face with a big dun horse who nickered eagerly to him.

Ebony pranced up to the dun and thrust out his muzzle. Their noses touched briefly. Black Lady nickered a warning, though she wasn't really worried about her son. Ebony realized at once that here was a horse different from the wild mares who bit and kicked if he ventured too close to one of them, and from the gray stallion who bossed the herd and who only tolerated the colt. Ebony moved closer to the gelding and sniffed at his rough coat of grayish-brown hair. Charlie reached out and ran his teeth along the colt's neck. The teeth felt good as they scratched Ebony's neck.

At that moment Big Baldy noticed what was going

on. Black Lady was moving toward the pair, nickering eagerly. Big Baldy screamed savagely and
charged down the slope with bared teeth, his ears
flattened, forefeet lifting high and smashing down
on the ground. Ebony whirled around and pivoted
as Charlie snorted and fled. Big Baldy pounded past
the colt and his mother. His fury was frightening,

but he wasn't able to catch up with Charlie, who was skimming along swiftly over the tall grass and clumps of rose briar. Big Baldy wasted his breath screaming and finally slowed to a trot as he returned to the knoll where he had been standing guard. He was still very angry, but there wasn't much he could do about it. He just couldn't catch the dun.

Black Lady knew she had better get back into the herd before the stallion thought of punishing her for straying off and meeting the gelding. She trotted into the herd with Ebony at her side, reaching the safety of herd while Big Baldy was still watching Charlie.

Most of the days were sunny and hot, but usually a shower blew up in the afternoon which would last a half hour or so. These showers kept the slopes green and lush. They made the mountain daisies, the blue lupine, and the columbines thrive and put on a riot of blossoms.

During an afternoon shower one day Big Baldy sighted a couple of riders. He watched them from a high ridge and decided that they had picked up the trail of his herd. The shower had turned to a heavy drizzle, so they would not be able to follow the trail far. But seeing them move up the slope made him decide to leave the high country above Boiling Springs Ranch.

Big Baldy always had escape routes leading away

from any bench or mesa where he grazed his herd. A steep arroyo led down from the bench where the mares were now feeding. It dropped into a narrow canyon which climbed up into rough barren country.

Big Baldy whirled and screamed his stampede signal. The mares were instantly alert; they crowded together and plunged toward the arroyo. None of them wanted to bring up the rear and feel the sharp teeth of the stallion. Black Lady could not use her full speed because of Ebony. She and the other three mares with colts took most of the punishment meted out by the gray stallion. She was the only one who lashed out at him with her hind feet, so she fared better than the other mothers. Ebony was frightened and stayed as close to his mother's side as he could. Her lashing hoofs protected him from Big Baldy.

Up on the bench, Charlie ran to the head of the arroyo and stopped, watching the mares plunging down the slippery trail. His ears slanted forward and he shook his head. Below him the tightly packed mass of horses slipped and skidded. The lead mare went down and was badly battered before she could regain her footing. Finally Charlie moved into the arroyo. He was sure-footed, and he did not try to move fast. Once he reached the canyon bed below, he would trail the herd and catch up with them.

Major Howard's riders pulled up at the rim of the arroyo. Tex, the Bar T foreman, slapped water from his hat and scowled. He was a tall thin man who had spent most of his life in the saddle. He knew cows and he knew horses.

"Don't know how they do it without breaking their legs and necks," he said.

McLarin, a youngster in years but a good horseman, laughed. "If you had that gray devil chewing on your hip pocket, you'd do it."

"Four shod mares with him," Hank Gilly, the Bar T horse breaker, said. He had been studying the hoof prints in the soft earth.

"We'll let them go," Tex said. "But one of these days I'll get that gray boss in my sights." He swung his horse around and they all headed back across the bench.

Tex's threat was mostly for the benefit of the others. Major Howard had ordered his men to shoot the gray stallion. He didn't want the wild mares eating his grass, but most of all he didn't want Big Baldy stealing any of his valuable mares. Tex was against shooting a horse, even a scrub or a raider. Secretly he admired Big Baldy, knowing that he was an extraordinary horse.

By the time the herd had climbed up into the breaks, the sky was clear except for a towering thunderhead which lifted its fleecy crest high above the peaks of the Crazy Kill Mountains. Lightning stabbed out of the black underbelly of the cloud, and thunder rumbled and echoed along the cliff walls. Ebony's eyes rolled and he pressed against his mother's side. This was the first heavy thunder he had ever heard.

In this high wasteland there were many uptilted ledges of barren rock with much brush crowding out the grass. But there was grass and there were many small streams fed by snow which was still melting on the peaks above timber line. The air was cool and clear with deep blue sky overhead. This was a place where bull elk and mule deer bucks came in summer to nurse their growing antlers. Here, there were few flies to attack the spongy blood-filled structures which would later become hardened lances of bone, antlers which would be the weapons of the bulls and the bucks when the fall mating season arrived.

Ebony had never seen a bull elk or a buck deer. He had seen a few does and fawns but never one of the family that had antlers. He was interested in the first big bull he met. The old fellow was feeding in a meadow close to a spring which emptied into a basin of marshy ground. The bull had two smaller companions. If this had been fall, Ebony's life would have been in danger, but it was summer now and the bulls were meek and shy. When the colt walked up to the big fellow, he shied away. Even so small a horse might injure his tender antlers.

Black Lady quickly called her son away from the

big elk. He did not obey at once; he was beginning
to have a mind of his own. Having the elk give
ground made him feel very brave. Here was a huge
animal who was afraid of him. He danced away
from the elk and kicked up his heels, then whinnied
as loudly as he could.

A half mile farther on, the herd passed four mule
deer bucks. They were bunched together in a peaceful and friendly gathering, content to lie in the open
where no low branch could disfigure the tender
growth on their heads. Later they would meet as
deadly enemies, but now all they wanted to do was
to fill their bellies with tender shoots and juicy stems,
to build up fat and to nourish their fast-growing
weapons. This would take a lot of fodder because the
antlers grew amazingly fast. In one short summer
they would grow from mere hair-covered knobs to
great racks of bone.

The breaks offered protection from man. No
range riders ever came that way, because no cattle
or horses ranged there. Major Howard's men would
not bother the herd as long as the horses stayed off
the Bar T range. The cougars were aware that they
were safe from men with rifles, so were the wolves
and the bears. The breaks played host to a variety
of hunters and hunted.

One surly old bear was king of the mountain.
Clubfoot had been boss of the breaks for a number

of years. He was the biggest black bear in the country and he was filled with hatred for other bears. He drove them out of his territory or killed them if he could catch them. He had long since lost any desire to seek a mate in the spring. Two young bears—brothers—had invaded his territory that spring and Clubfoot was constantly on the lookout for them. One was a brown and the other a black.

Ebony met Clubfoot while the herd was feeding near an aspen grove, a spot the big bear often visited. At that high altitude there were few such groves. When Ebony sighted the bear he was marking a tree with his teeth, standing on his hind legs to reach up as high as he could, then slashing a gash in the soft green bark. This was his way of telling the world he was king. No other bear could put his mark higher on a trunk than Clubfoot. The mark warned any wandering bear to beware. He growled and rumbled as he bit into the bark.

Black Lady was feeding below the aspen grove out of sight of the bear. Ebony trotted up the hill and halted to stare at the strange animal standing erect against the aspen tree. An instinct of fear stirred in him, a warning that here was a dangerous creature. But the warning was not strong enough to make him whirl and run away. He was separated by years from horses who met bears and knew about them. He nickered and stamped one foot upon the ground. This shaggy creature might run away as the bull elk had.

Clubfoot turned away from the tree and dropped to all fours. His eyesight wasn't very good, so he had to stretch his neck and stare hard to make sure there was a small horse close to him. Tough as he was, he avoided horses guarded by a wild stallion. When he was satisfied that this was a colt and that he was alone, he growled loudly and charged, his jaws open wide, baring teeth which were still sharp.

Ebony suddenly realized that he was in trouble. He whinnied wildly as he whirled to flee. His call was answered at once by his mother. Clubfoot was so aroused and his roar so loud that he did not hear the mare's answer. He was intent upon overtaking the colt and smashing him with a paw which had felled more than one elk.

On a downhill run Clubfoot could move fast. He quickly closed the gap between himself and Ebony, reared up, and raised a huge paw. But he did not strike. Before he could leap in close enough to smash the colt, he was faced by a charging black mare and he heard the scream of the herd stallion answering Black Lady's frantic calls for help. He slid to a halt and shifted to meet the mare's attack, rising up and flailing the air with his paws like a boxer. Black Lady acted purely by instinct, her courage backed by mother love. She swerved and a big paw armed with long claws missed her shoulder by inches. Clubfoot now realized that he had made a mistake in attacking the colt, but a great fury filled him. He would kill this horse. He aimed another blow but Black Lady danced back, her forefeet lashing out; then she whirled and let fly with her hind feet. Her reach was longer than the bear's. Both hoofs smashed into the flailing paws. Clubfoot roared in fury and tried to close in.

Big Baldy arrived on the scene and leaped at the bear, teeth bared, hoofs pounding. Clubfoot's anger changed to caution. He decided to retreat. He turned and started up the slope at a lumbering gallop. Black Lady raced away to where Ebony stood watching, but Big Baldy charged after the bear. His teeth sank into the shaggy rump. Clubfoot bawled loudly and leaped aside, then reared up and lashed out. His blows were met by the hoofs of the stallion. Big Baldy had the power and the weight; his blows almost sent Clubfoot over on his back. Clubfoot had not climbed a tree in years, but he knew he had to climb one now or be battered to pulp. He backed toward a big aspen, fending off Big Baldy's blows as best he could. When he reached the tree, he leaped around it and started to climb. Big Baldy's teeth made the bear pull himself upward faster than he had ever climbed a tree in his youth, tearing big wads of hair out of the bear's rump and ripping

gashes in the tough hide. Clubfoot wedged himself in a crotch of the tree and roared his defiance at the stallion.

Black Lady and Ebony moved upward cautiously when they saw that Big Baldy had routed the bear. They halted and stood watching the big fellow circle the tree, stamping and screaming. Finally Big Baldy turned away and loped down the hill. Black Lady started running toward the herd. Big Baldy stayed close behind her, nipping her sharply every time he caught up with her. He was punishing her for straying so far away from the other mares. Ebony ran as fast as he could, but he was left behind. His mother paid no attention to his frantic whinnying. She knew he was no longer in danger and she wanted to get away from Big Baldy's teeth.

Ebony and his mother were to get into trouble many times before she learned that she must stay close to the other mares. One evening they strayed away from the herd, lured by lush grass growing close to a thicket which bordered a stand of spruce and pine. No wild mare would have ventured close to such a thicket at dusk or at dawn. They would have known that it could hide one or more killers.

This thicket did hide a killer. A big tom cougar had been watching the herd for over an hour. Like all cougars he could be patient, and like all cougars he prized horsemeat highly. He would pass up a doe any time to get a fat colt. But experience had taught him that it was not safe to attack a colt in a herd. The herd stallion, even though he might be a scrub, was always alert and never very far from his mares. And any stallion was dangerous. So the cougar had lain watching Big Baldy and his mares, waiting for a mare and colt to leave the herd.

The cougar's patience was rewarded when Black Lady and Ebony moved away from the other mares and started toward the thicket, cropping grass, then moving and stopping to crop again. He was stretched out on a ledge above the meadow where the horses were feeding. Flattening his belly to the ground, he circled until he was above the thicket, then started creeping slowly toward it, using the thicket as a shield to hide his stealthy approach.

Black Lady halted at a large clump of bunch grass fifteen yards from the thicket and started nipping off the tender stems. Ebony wasn't hungry, but he was filled with eager energy. He danced away from his mother and shied sharply, pretending to be frightened by a tall stand of skunk cabbage.

Two yellow eyes watched Ebony from inside the thicket. The cougar lay motionless except for the black tip of his tail. That was raised like a flag and jerked back and forth. It was his way of warning any other cougar that might be creeping toward the thicket that this kill was staked out. His powerful hind legs were pulled up under him, their muscles taut as steel springs.

Out in the meadow, Ebony suddenly danced away from the skunk cabbage, kicked up his hind feet and dashed back to his mother. This was a game of make believe. He was pretending to escape from a dangerous enemy. Black Lady lifted her head and nickered softly. Ebony whirled and lashed out at her with his small hoofs, then dashed across the meadow, circling around as he ran. He widened the circle until he was running close to the edge of the park. His course took him past the thicket where the cougar lay.

The big cat set himself to spring. His timing would be precise, his aim accurate. With close to two hundred pounds of muscle and bone behind it the leap would carry terrific impact. One long high spring would place him on the colt's back. One paw armed with long curving claws would snap the colt's head back and break his neck. The cougar had already selected a tree to climb when the mare charged in as he knew she would. He could wait up in the tree until the mare gave up trying to rouse her son and left his body to join the herd. Then he would leap down and feast upon tender horsemeat. His long body shot up and out in a mighty leap.

In his frisky mood Ebony wanted lots of action. He bounded aside as he passed the thicket. It was not because he saw the yellow body rising above the

tops of the buck brush, it was all a part of the game
he was playing. His leap to one side saved his life.
The cougar had no way of knowing the little horse
would suddenly bounce aside. He landed in the
grass, and the force of his leap carried him several
yards out into the meadow before he could stop and
whirl around. Ebony saw him and started whinnying loudly, this time with real fright.

Black Lady answered with a wild cry, then
charged to the rescue of her son. Her call for help
was answered by Big Baldy. The cougar was not a
killer who let anger or fury dull his wits as had the
old black bear. For a second or two he considered
his chances of striking down the colt before the mare
could reach him. But Ebony was fleeing across the
meadow and the chase would take the killer away
from the timber where he knew he could easily escape from the mare and the stallion, who was now
closing in. He snarled defiantly, then leaped toward
the thicket. A second bound carried him to the edge
of the timber, a third took him to the base of a tall
pine. He climbed the tree swiftly and flattened himself on a limb.

Big Baldy arrived and circled the tree. His fury
was great and he screamed loudly, but the cat was
well out of his reach, teeth bared, tail lashing. So
Big Baldy gave his attention to Black Lady who had
headed back to the herd. He raced after her with
bared teeth, but she outran him and reached the

herd before he could nip her flanks. Ebony was already among the mares. They lifted their heads, and realizing the big stallion might vent his fury on them, they whirled and charged away across the meadow. Big Baldy thundered after them, screaming loudly. The run turned into a stampede which took the herd deep into the pines above the meadow. Big Baldy had to be satisfied with taking his wrath out on the slower mares.

Spring was a time of plenty in the high country for all living things. The predators had easy hunting; the hunted had an abundance of things to eat. The white famine of snow time was forgotten for a while. Growing things hastened to put on blossoms which could turn to seed before the fall frosts arrived. Seed and nut gatherers rushed about to their storage holes, the chips filling their cheek pouches with seeds. Squirrels littered the ground around their hidden logs with the husks of pine cones from which they had removed the kernels. Their small bins inside hollow trees began to fill with nuts. Other animals ate and filled a different kind of granary with food for winter. The bears and many other animals stored their food in the form of layers of fat under their skins. Big Baldy and his herd grew sleek and fat. There were now eight colts; only four of the mares were barren. Ebony grew rapidly, his awkward legs took on a trim look and his small chest filled out. His mother no longer had to wait for him when Big Baldy sent the herd pounding down off a ridge or into a canyon.

Though the high country was usually pleasant in the summer it did have moods, some of them violent and wild, others gloomy. There were days when the sunny canyons and slopes were shrouded with gray mist and the ground was drenched with cold misty rain. The most spectacular of the mountain moods was the cloudburst, known to Westerners as the flash flood.

One afternoon the herd was grazing in a narrow canyon. A clear stream foamed over round boulders and fanned out into choppy riffles between the rough water and a sharp bend in the canyon. The walls on each side of the canyon were steep rims of rock on which a few pines and fir trees had managed to secure holds in crevices and pockets. A belt of tall grass no more than fifty feet at its widest, grew down to the willow fringe along the creek.

The day was sun-drenched with a deep blue sky overhead and a cool breeze flowing down from the peaks above. Ebony frisked with the other colts and fillies while their mothers cropped grass. Black Lady, as was her habit, grazed a little apart from the others. She had not yet accepted them completely. They, on their part, considered her a creature of man. The other three branded mares had been with

the herd long enough for the wild ones to have forgotten their past.

The colts raced about kicking up their heels. In a
sudden burst of energy they all dashed away down
the stream. Ebony, being the fastest runner, was in
the lead by ten lengths as they approached the sharp
bend in the canyon. The other colts halted suddenly
when their mothers whinnied a warning, and
wheeled about to return to the herd.

Ebony halted, but he did not turn back. Charlie
was standing just around the bend where Big Baldy
could not see him. Charlie's ears slanted forward in
a friendly manner and the sun glinted on his dun-
colored back. Ebony nickered eagerly and galloped
around the bend to join his friend. He shouldered
against the gelding and Charlie scratched his small
hips with his teeth, digging gently at the root of
Ebony's kinky tail. The teeth acted like a rough-
toothed curry comb, loosening dust and dead hair.

The two horses were visiting, not paying attention to anything around them, when a deep rumble
of thunder echoed along the canyon walls. Charlie
looked up into the sky, but Ebony paid no attention
to the thunder; he heard it almost every day. A big
black cloud had rolled in over the watershed which
fed the creek. Below its black underside a gray wall
of rain descended to the slope. Charlie nickered uneasily, his eyes on the cloud.

Up the slope, above the canyon, the cloud had

literally opened and was pouring a deluge of water upon the rocky ground. The volume was so great that little water sank into the earth; it swept down the steep slope toward the creek, building up volume and depth as it rushed along until a solid wall of water was plunging down into the clear stream. The force of the rushing torrent uprooted trees and loosened big boulders which bounded downward amid the broken trees and other debris, the whole forming a dirty brown mass laced with white foam. By the time the flood reached the creek it was a roaring monster ten feet high at its face. It filled the narrow canyon from wall to wall.

The roar of the descending water filled the narrow gorge. Big Baldy screamed a warning and charged upon his herd. There was no hope of outrunning the water—the only avenue of escape was the steep wall of the canyon. With slashing hoofs and snapping teeth, he sent the mares and colts toward the wall. Black Lady looked around wildly for her son. She could not see him. Big Baldy lashed at her flank, and she plunged up over a big boulder and pawed her way to a ledge which angled upward. Below her a mare lost her footing and plunged back into the tall grass. Two colts struggled vainly to climb a sheer face of rock. The mare was struggling to her feet, and the two colts were frantically leaping up against the wall when the wall of water and debris struck them. The mare was swept away kicking and struggling. The two colts were sucked into a whirlpool which dragged them down into the muddy depths.

Around the bend below, Charlie went into action. He shouldered Ebony up onto a ledge and leaped up beside him. Pushing and shouldering, he forced the terrified colt upward. The bend in the canyon saved them. The solid granite hurled the water back and sent it surging against the far wall. The mass of water passed so close to the pair that a big pine tree rising out of the flood raked Charlie's side with its torn branches. It twisted into the air like a tortured thing, hanging there a moment as though trying to get a grip upon the face of the cliff. Then it plunged from sight.

Charlie and Ebony did not move until the flood started to recede. Even after the mud-caked grass below began to show, Charlie made no move to descend; instead he started up along the ledge. Ebony followed him, keeping very close to the big dun's tail. He nickered eagerly for his mother, but he felt safe with the big gelding close to him.

Ebony might never have found his mother if Charlie hadn't led him to a meadow on a bench above the canyon where the herd had stopped to rest. Charlie was wise, he knew where to look. He halted in the timber close to a grass park and watched Ebony gallop down to meet his mother. He did not dare go any closer. Big Baldy was standing on a knoll close to his herd, his head was up, and he was very alert. The escape out of the canyon had keyed him up, and the tension had not left him.

Ebony nuzzled against his mother's flank and started nursing. She whinnied eagerly and rubbed her muzzle against his side. The flash flood was not forgotten, but fear of it had vanished like a shadow passing across a sunny meadow. That is the way of the wild. After hunters are out of sight the hunted creature loses its fear. With the hunter gone, panic ceases and only an alert watchfulness remains.

The colts started frolicking again, unaware that two of their number had been swallowed by the deluge. The mares began grazing. Big Baldy relaxed and started cropping grass. Charlie wandered off to find a clearing where he, too, could graze.

White Famine

INDIAN SUMMER cast her warm cloak over valley, canyon, and slope. In the foothills the scrub oak brush turned flaming red and covered the hills like a great rug of knobby carpeting. The aspens, cottonwoods, and willows formed masses of yellow and gold. The streams were bordered by a brilliant band of colorful willows. The mounds of color formed by the aspen groves stood out against the deep green of the conifers above them. Frost had not as yet turned the shrubs and the grass to dead brown, so the scene was full of color.

Ebony was now seven months of age. He was husky and full of life; everything about him indicated that he would grow up to be a great black

44

stallion like his father, Midnight. With Black Lady's blood lines added to his father's he could not fail to become a magnificent horse. He had begun to stay away from Big Baldy. The scarred old leader seemed to sense that the black colt would one day have to be dealt with, smashed and driven out of the herd or killed. That is the way with a wild herd.

Ebony paid less attention to Black Lady's fretting over him which became more lax as the days passed. But he still grazed close to her side at times. He sought out Charlie, and they often ran together. The colt could not match the old race horse's speed, but Charlie liked to have the youngster challenge him and Ebony enjoyed the wild dashes across a meadow. It was different from galloping around with the other colts and fillies. With Charlie it was a straight-away run, a race, something Charlie had been trained to do by the Lazy Y horse wrangler.

Big Baldy still flew into a rage when he sighted Charlie, often chasing him, but he was no longer concerned about the black stallion's habit of wandering away from the herd. He no longer felt an urge to protect the colt. Black Lady sometimes nickered to Ebony in an attempt to get him to come back, but she seldom followed him, and if she did, she never went far. With feed in abundance, her memory of the ranch dimmed. She still wasn't a tough wild mare; she would never learn the restless wariness of the wild mares, which was something they had been born with, but she now accepted Big Baldy as her lord and master.

During these last warm days, the creatures of Ebony's world were keyed to frantic efforts. The chickarees spent all of their time cutting cones from the tall pines, dashing to the ground to shuck them out and store away the nuts. The chips and the golden-mantled ground squirrels were busy. The old king bear was well padded with heavy layers of fat and had called a truce in his war upon the young brothers. He did not care to dissipate his stored fat in an effort to destroy them. He would renew the war when spring came. For the moment, he busied himself adding a few more pounds of energy.

The two brothers had separated. They were growing up and now treated each other as strangers. Ebony often saw them on the slopes or in the timber.

They were lazy fellows, the brown bear being lazier than his brother. He liked to prop his back against a tree and snooze, keeping just alert enough so that if Old Clubfoot appeared, he could make off. Now that the king had stopped hunting him he was lazier than ever, and he was rolling fat. The black brother was more curious about things and more active. But they both could go into action with surprising speed if the occasion called for it.

One day Ebony and Charlie were off for a run through the woods. They came to a small clearing in the pines and saw the black bear trotting along beside a fallen pine tree. Charlie halted; he was wary of bears, even small ones. He jerked up his head and uttered a warning nicker. Ebony stopped beside him to watch the bear. The fallen tree was a giant three feet through at the butt, the victim of old age and a violent wind storm. Suddenly the black bear bounded into the air, jumping cleanly over the tree trunk. He smashed his paws at something on the far side of the tree. Then a snowshoe rabbit darted away from the tree and into a thicket. The black bear reared up and looked around, pretending not to see the two horses as he ambled away.

At that moment Ebony spotted another bear. The brown brother was sitting with his back against a tree, sunning himself and napping, about twenty yards above the ambling black bear. The black bear paused and looked at his brother, then started circling cautiously. When he was above him, with the tree between himself and his brother, he crept forward. Ebony and Charlie watched with interest. The black reached the tree without disturbing his brother. Reaching around it, he whacked his brother hard and woofed loudly. The brown exploded, leaping away from the tree, tumbling end over end across the grass until he finally got his feet under him and bounded away. The black bear, looking innocent, ambled away.

Every creature was fat, including the horses. Nature had been kind to them during the summer. But the period of feasting was about over. One night a heavy frost came, not a white hoar frost which had been covering the grass with white crystals every night; this was black frost, killing cold, and it froze the sap in the grass stems and the flower stalks. In one night the meadows lost their bright green color and within days the landscape was brown and bare. One afternoon a heavy wind swept over the mountain and whipped the leaves from the aspens, willows, and cottonwood. They swirled to the ground in red and golden clouds and eddied into windrows of color. The silver trunks of the aspens lifted naked arms to the sky. Only the spruce, the pines, and the hemlocks remained green and unchanged.

The does and the cow elks were moving toward

lower valleys, traveling slowly, lingering where the forage was good. Up in the high country, the bull elk and the bucks began to grow restless. Their antlers were now hard lances of bone which they raked through bushes or rubbed against trees to remove the last of the hairy velvet from the bone. The males were now hostile; they no longer lay down meekly with each other, but stalked about alone. At evening the bugling of the big bulls echoed along the cliffs and rang down the slopes. This was a new sound to Ebony and the fierce high call, which always ended in a series of snorting coughs, stirred the black stallion and made him prance about.

Big Baldy became as restless as the bulls and the bucks, but for a different reason. There was a feeling in the air which he did not like, a warning of things to come. One day he started his herd down toward the sheltered valleys below. The big stallion did not set a fast pace, like the does and elk cows. He did not hurry. Ebony stayed ahead, well away from the surly old stallion. Charlie went along, usually above the mares, always keeping them in sight.

The herd finally came to a snug valley which suited Big Baldy. There was tall grass in a big meadow, willows along a stream, and many groves of sweet-bark cottonwoods. A ridge ran along the southern border of the valley. The deer and the elk also recognized this valley as a good place to winter. There was room for all, and the valley was sheltered on three sides by high ridges and rims. The herd entered through a narrow canyon. At the lower end of the valley another canyon cut through the long ridge and offered an exit.

The bull elks and the buck mule deer also came down from the high country, each ready to battle for the favor of the cows and does. Like knights of old, they marched down from the rims and ridges, necks swollen, eyes filled with angry fire.

Ebony watched his first battle between bulls early one evening when a flaming sunset filled the sky with a rosy glow reflected from fleecy clouds. He had strayed away from the herd and was standing at the edge of a clearing.

Here a half dozen cow elk were feeding. There were several husky calves with them and one a late calf which was very young. It had bedded down near a bush close to the upper edge of the park. As Ebony watched, a big bull marched out of the timber and strode toward the cows. He was a great fellow with a fine rack of antlers, and as he came forward he thrust his muzzle out and laid his antlers back. Suddenly, the stillness of the evening was shattered by a bugling call from above. The cows lifted their heads, but otherwise showed no interest in the approaching bull or the one calling from the ridge above. The bull was only a few yards from the cows when the challenge rang out. He halted and lifted his head, then sent a savage call ringing back to the unseen bull. His bugle was answered by another which came from the timber close above the clearing.

When the challenger stepped into the open, he

halted and the two bulls stood staring at each other, grunting savagely. The intruder was almost as big as the first bull but not so old. The fall before he had been a squealer who hadn't mastered mature bugle calls and could only utter a squealing sound when he was aroused. Now he was a mature bull and ready to claim his share of the cows scattered over the valley.

The two bulls marched toward each other with antlers lowered. For a few yards they seemed in no hurry, then both leaped forward in a lunging charge. They came together with a jarring impact that sounded like the crack of a pistol. Each parried thrusts which were meant to sink knives of bone into the vitals of the other. For a time they shoved and grunted, each trying to shake the other off balance. Both fought by instinct—the young bull in his first battle knew what to do as well as the old bull who had fought many battles. Finally they backed off and stood blowing while they recovered their breath. Then they charged again and came together with thudding impact. Ebony watched, his ears pricked forward. The fierce struggling excited him. He moved a little closer. In their struggle the bulls covered considerable ground. They passed around and over the calf which was curled up close to a thicket. True to its training, the calf did not move and by some chance none of the big hoofs struck it.

The bulls made charge after charge after charge; their mouths sagged open and their sides heaved with the effort. Finally the young bull was forced backward. He was weakening under the savage attack of the bigger bull. Once he slipped to his knees but was able to struggle back to his feet. At the next charge he missed his footing and lunged sidewise. This exposed his flank and the old bull drove his antlers deep into the side of the youngster. The young bull was hurled on his side. He staggered to his feet, but he could not get his legs set before the old bull lunged again. He went down again, and this time he could not get his feet under him. The old bull grunted triumphantly as he stabbed at his helpless rival; then he backed away and turned to claim his harem. Minutes later, the young bull got to his feet and staggered into the timber where he lay down. He was defeated, but he was still defiant. His angry grunts were evidence that he would live to battle again.

The fights between the bucks were of a similar pattern. Some ended in mortal wounds, but mostly the defeated one made off to look for does elsewhere. One pair locked their antlers so securely that they could not pull them apart. They lay locked together for days and finally starved to death, with a pair of coyotes waiting for the end while a dozen buzzards circled in the air and watched, alighting when the coyotes moved in to finish the weakened bucks.

The first big storm found Big Baldy's herd at the upper end of the valley. The day had dawned clear with blue skies overhead. A breeze blowing up from the sage-covered hills below brought with it the smell of the desert and warm air rising from the mesas far to the south. Ebony filled his belly with the ripe grass while the sun beat upon the thick coat of hair which he had recently acquired against the coming of winter. Then he wandered up into the narrow canyon leading into the valley. The music of a stream filled the air and a raven flapped overhead lazily, heading south. A wedge of geese swept over, also heading south. They were honkers and their cries filtered downward as they passed overhead. Ebony did not notice them. He did not understand what the flight meant. No warning stirred in him to tell him that it was time to leave the north country.

He moved on and halted at the upper edge of a beaver pond. A dozen beavers, the entire colony, were busy stripping limbs from aspen trees they had felled the night before or cutting the trees into lengths they could move down to the pond. Had a woodsman observed them he would have been convinced that the winter would be a hard one. An old beaver who seemed to be the boss or leader of four young beavers was pulling at the end of a large log. His four helpers pulled and pushed, too. Their efforts were not well organized; two were pulling against the other. The log was wedged behind a big boulder, and even the old beaver did not seem to know what to do about it. Suddenly the four young beavers got together in their efforts and the log bounced over the rock, bowling the old beaver over on his back. He scrambled to his feet and slapped his flat tail on the ground, then bounded after the log which was now rolling down toward the pond.

Ebony walked to the edge of the pond and lowered his head to drink. The water was muddy and flavored with aspen sap and decayed weeds and brush. He snorted and turned away. At the sound of his snort, a beaver out in the pond slapped his tail on the water making a sound like the explosion of a gun. The beaver dived as did two others swimming near-by. Ripples wavered away from the spot toward shore.

Under the muddy water, the beavers had piled up a big supply of limbs and trunks, all anchored to the muddy bottom securely. Safe in their mud-thatched lodges, they would be snug during the winter with an ample supply of food stored in their pond. Once the mud roofs froze they would be as well protected against predators as if they had iron shields over their heads.

Ebony trotted on. Once he whinnied for Charlie and was answered from a cottonwood grove a hundred yards above. Charlie was seeking a big grove of sweet-bark cottonwoods where he could be comfortable during the time of deep snow, which he knew was coming.

Ebony moved up toward the grove. He had only gone a little way when the wind changed. It began funneling down the canyon from the peaks above. Ebony walked out into a small meadow. Overhead gray clouds began fanning out over the granite spires of the Crazy Kill peaks. The clouds settled down and scudded along the rims of the canyon filling it with gray mist. Ebony halted and sniffed deeply. Here was something new, a different smell to the air. The new breeze was chilly. The descending clouds made him uneasy. Suddenly the air

around him was filled with big white flakes of snow.
They floated down in a swirling mass and vanished
when they hit the ground which was still well above
freezing temperature.

The young stallion whinnied again and this time
his answer was Charlie himself. He trotted out of the
cottonwood grove and stood shaking his head and
tossing his mane. As Ebony started to trot across the
dead grass to meet his friend, a blast of icy wind
struck him, and almost instantly the big flakes were
replaced by fine, powder-dry snow which stung his
muzzle like driven sand. The fine snow was riding
a howling wind. Instinctively Ebony turned his back
to the blast. Charlie shouldered against the colt and
tried to get him to move against the storm into the
cottonwood grove. Ebony wanted no part of the
stinging blast. He headed down country with his
tail to the wind. Charlie lowered his head and
moved into the wind and snow toward the cottonwood grove. He knew it would furnish shelter from
the blizzard.

Ebony moved along at a trot, his head lowered.
He kept on down the canyon. drifting with the
storm. He was shut in by a wall of whiteness and
could see no landmarks by which he could guide his
course. The only trees he saw were those he almost
bumped into. Reducing his speed to a walk, he
plodded along as snow began to pile up back of

rocks and fallen logs. He whinnied loudly as he moved along, but he got no answer. Finally he found himself in a cottonwood grove bordered by heavy willow growth along one side. The willows and the cottonwoods broke the force of the storm. Ebony moved close to the willow windbreak and halted. He stood with his head down and shook snow from his mane and back.

As the storm howled on, darkness settled. It screamed through the bare branches overhead and snow sifted down and began to pile up on the ground. Ebony discovered that he was hungry. In spite of this strange white terror, his stomach was calling for food. But the grass was now covered with snow. He reached out and started nibbling twigs. They were sweet and tasted good. He was safe; he was sheltered from the blizzard and he had food. But he was still uneasy, because he was alone. He whinnied from time to time, but his call was smothered by the howling wind.

The blizzard raged for two days and two nights. It dumped four feet of snow on the valley, much of it blown into deep drifts. Parts of the meadows and parks remained clear, where the wind had swept the snow away. Ebony had stamped out a small circle in the snow so that he could more easily reach the limbs of several young cottonwood trees. He enlarged the circle as he cleaned up the twigs around him. He ate snow when he was thirsty and his thick winter coat shielded him against the bitter cold which followed the storm. If it had not been for a gnawing loneliness, he would have been content, but he was bothered because he had never been away from the herd.

The third day dawned cold and clear. Ebony's breath plumed out around his head and formed frost on his forelock. After the light came, he browsed a little, calling a few times, then started off to look for the herd. He plunged through the deep loose snow in the grove and came to an open meadow. Avoiding the deeper snow, he broke into a gallop, heading out across the valley. When he was halfway across he sighted the herd. The mares had moved out on the wind-swept ridge below where the grass was swept clear of snow. Big Baldy was standing guard on high ground. Ebony's mother was cropping grass at the lower edge of the herd. With an eager whinny, he galloped up the slope toward her. She saw him coming and answered briefly. Her main interest at the moment was the rich dry grass. Feeding on cottonwood twigs and bark was not to her liking. With the whole herd crowded into one grove she had not been able to get her share of fodder. The wild mares had savagely protected the parts they picked for feeding, and Black Lady had fared badly.

White famine had struck the high country. When the days were clear, the cold was bitter and when the wind blew, fine snow swirled up and filled the air as

completely as when a storm was going on. Some of the dwellers were snug and safe. The old king bear slept in a cave with snow blocking the entrance and keeping out the cold and wind. The shiftless brothers found shelter when the storm came. They were back together, cuddled up inside a hollow tree. They lay close together and licked the inside of their forepaws when they occasionally half awakened.

The chips and the squirrels had their stored food,

the mice and rats burrowed deep under the snow
and dug for roots. The rabbits found cover by bur-
rowing into snow which had drifted deep in the
willows along the creek. They came out to feed on
willow bark and stems, but they seldom moved more
than a foot or two from their burrows. It was the
killers—the wolves, coyotes, bobcats, and cougars—
who suffered a real threat of starvation. The cougar
sank into the deep snow and lost his speed, as did all
of the other killers. They could not overtake the
snowshoe rabbits whose big furry feet served as
snowshoes. Nor the deer whose slim hoofs cut
through the snow and allowed them to bound along
as fast as they did when there was no snow. There
were no thickets to offer them stalking cover; the
cottontails could spot them a long way off and duck
into their holes. The only killer who got along fairly
well was the Canada lynx, a big cat who has large
furry feet like the snowshoe rabbit.

A pair of cougars and an old she-wolf and her
three sons took to hanging around the horse herd
and the groves where the elk had formed yards,
waiting for a weakened animal to stray away from
the others. There were such members in the horse
herd and among the elk, young animals who found
it hard to reach browse, and old animals who had
failed to build up fat during the summer. Once
down, the killers could easily finish them, or if they

did not go down, the wolves or the cougars would pull them down.

The killers had better luck with the elk than with the horses. The bulls had ceased to be aggressive and were now only interested in eating. Like the buck deer, they had used up so much energy during the fall that they had gone into the winter in poor condition. Also, they were about to drop their antlers. Protecting the young was now left to the old cows. With the horse herd it was different. Big Baldy would smash any killer that attacked even a weakling. But when a mare or a colt went down and was left behind when the herd moved on, the killers feasted. The four wolves finally gave all of their attention to the elk while one big tom cougar stayed with the horses. The other big cougar foraged for rabbits and dug into the snow to uncover mice and wood rats.

Ebony stayed fairly close to his mother, but he fared better than she did. Raised where she had always had shelter from winter storms and a feed rack filled with hay, she did not know how to cope with winter conditions in the wilds. She soon began to weaken; she lost weight and as her strength waned, she was less able to forage. During storms the herd was forced to seek shelter in groves and to live on cottonwood bark and limbs. This was Black Lady's worst time. On clear days she was able to get some grass, though the wild mares usually guarded the best patches of open ground.

Among the smaller killers life was as hard as with the big ones. The weasel tribe hunted constantly but often went hungry for days. The biggest member of this family was the wolverine, rare in these mountains and usually a drifter from the north. Carcajou was a killer more ruthless and bloodthirsty than his smaller kin, and he weighed up to thirty pounds as compared to a weasel's half pound. During the winter famine Carcajou would attack any animal he met.

Ebony met Carcajou one bleak afternoon while the herd was feeding on the ridge. The uncovered grass made a narrow strip a half mile in length along the ridge near its crest. Big Baldy was becoming increasingly more antagonistic toward the little black stallion. His temper was always bad, and it got worse as the rigors of winter used up his reserves of fat. Ebony stayed well away from him at all times, and he did not mix with the mares because Big Baldy might corner him there.

He was feeding at the lower end of the strip with Black Lady when Carcajou, his small eyes glaring out across the white world, came loping along the slope. He had not made a kill for five days, and his belly was lank and cramped with hunger. He looked a little like a cub bear as he bounded along. (In his northern home he is often called skunk bear because of his looks and the fact that he carries a musk which rivals that of a skunk.) His eyes were not very strong, and the glare from the snow did not help them, but he saw movement when Black Lady shifted to a spot a little distance from Ebony. Ebony was easy to see against the snow as was his mother, but it was the movement which attracted Carcajou.

Carcajou bounded down the slope snarling as he ran. Even when well fed he did not know what fear was. In his time he had driven cougars and wolves from their kills. No animal wanted to tangle with a demon who would die ripping and clawing before he would break away from a fight. Ebony saw the squat beast coming and heard his savage snarls. He whinnied loudly and dashed to his mother's side where he whirled around to face the attacker. Black Lady called wildly for help before she galloped away. Ebony turned to follow her.

Carcajou was not a fast runner, but he was a persistent one. The time it took for Ebony to turn around gave the wolverine his chance. He leaped at the colt, landing on his shoulder where he hung slashing and clawing. Ebony screamed wildly and started to buck, then charged toward the herd. The startled mares moved together, and Ebony dashed into their midst. There was a wild melee as Big Baldy charged into the plunging mass of horses. Black Lady was now trying to help her son but could not get to him.

Big Baldy had never met a wolverine, but that

did not matter. His fury matched Carcajou's. Rearing up, he smashed at the wolverine. His blow
knocked the colt flat, but it also jarred the wolverine
off Ebony's back. Leaping up, Carcajou sprang at
the old stallion's muzzle which was lowered as Big
Baldy sought to use his teeth. Seeing the black fury

flying toward him, Big Baldy lashed out with his hoof again. One big hoof landed on the shoulder of the killer and sent him tumbling over and over down the slope. A deep drift fanning out back of a bush stopped him. He writhed and struggled to free himself so he could attack again.

The herd of mares was stampeding down the ridge. Big Baldy screamed loudly and galloped after them. Ebony was left behind to limp along as best he could. But he was able to put distance between himself and the wolverine because the wounded hunter had trouble digging himself out of the drift. By the time he was clear, Ebony was beyond range of his weak eyes.

Free of the drift Carcajou stood snarling and peering about him. He finally moved off up the ridge toward a stand of second-growth pines. Before daylight faded he met his fate, not in battle but in a way that often ends the career of desperately hungry killers.

Carcajou came to a pine sapling and halted. A porcupine was swaying in the branches above him, chewing bark and grunting to himself. He had no winter food problems because there was plenty of pine bark available. Generally he fed seated on the snow beside a young tree. In summer woodsmen could judge the depth of the previous winter's snow by the height of the girdling made by porcupines. Today Porky had felt like climbing.

Carcajou looked up at the gnawer, and his stomach cried out for meat. He climbed the sapling and knocked the porcupine out of the tree, then leaped down and pounced upon it. Disregarding the black-tipped arrows of quill, he tore at his victim and gulped down pieces of meat and skin. He was so ravenous that he ate every bit of his kill: hide, quills, and all. Unlike another of his tribe, the fisher, he did not bother to turn the porcupine over and attack his quill-less underbelly, scooping out the meat but leaving the hide.

Five days later the arrows of death worked their way into his vital organs. Their barbed points with backward-pointing spines made the arrows push deeper every time Carcajou moved. Carcajou ended his career of banditry and killing beside a fallen log where he snarled defiance to the world with his last breath.

The herd settled down to weather the ordeal of cold and blizzards. Ebony's wounds healed quickly. His shaggy coat had saved him from any deep slashes, so there would be no bad scars.

Ebony fared well enough, but Black Lady lost her interest in life. She made less and less of an effort to find grass or cottonwood and willow browse. One thing Ebony learned which contributed much to his education was added wariness. After the attack by the wolverine he was more alert. He was learning the things a wild horse had to know to survive.

Outcasts

ALONE in his cottonwood grove up near the canyon wall, Charlie was having real troubles. The wandering tom cougar discovered him and set about trying to make a kill. A lone horse was a lure he could not resist. In his desperate need for food he would attack even a big strong horse like Charlie. He was lean and gaunt, but he had lost none of his cunning. The way of the wolf was not his way. He would plan a stealthy approach. Even with hunger gnawing inside him, he had patience.

The big killer crept close to the cottonwood grove and flattened his tawny body on a flat rock which rose above the snow. His yellow color blended with the buff sandstone. His yellow eyes watched Charlie

69

as he stripped bark from a cottonwood limb. His vision was not clear because snow was swirling down among the trees. But the storm helped, since it kept Charlie in the grove. Never venturing out of the ridge when a blizzard was on, he had not left his shelter for two days.

The cougar checked everything. He checked the tree Charlie was feeding under, noting the limbs which would be strong enough to bear his weight but high enough up so that his drop would carry crushing impact. His eyes followed Charlie as he moved to another tree. He would select a tree and climb to a high limb, then lie there until the horse finally came to that tree. He could be patient; he had often stayed on a limb or a ledge watching a trail for days. The reward would be worth waiting for. The carcass of a horse would go a long way toward carrying him through the winter. The deep snow inside the grove ruled out a ground attack. Like the hoofs of the deer, Charlie's feet would sink into the snow and give him a foothold for running.

That afternoon the storm suddenly ended, sweeping on over the Crazy Kill range. The pale sun with two sun-dogs, pale spots of reflected light, riding beside it, shone on the vast expanse of new snow. Charlie moved out of the grove into a wind-swept park and started digging for grass. Out in the open the yellow killer had no chance to creep up on the horse. He leaped down from the rock and circled inside the grove, finally selecting a large cottonwood tree under which Charlie had tramped and packed the snow. He climbed it and stretched out on a big limb twenty feet above the ground. The cottonwood was almost in the center of the grove. Its lower branches swept downward, making it a good place for a horse to browse. The cougar would stay on the limb and wait for the horse to return to the grove. It might be that night or the next day, but he would be there ready to leap if the gelding passed close to the tree or halted under it.

That evening a cold wind started blowing and Charlie returned to the grove seeking a windbreak and a place to bed down. Wind combined with such bitter cold could chill even a horse protected by a winter coat. Charlie halted on the lee side of a thicket of alders growing just inside the grove. He stamped his feet and shook snow from his shaggy back and head. The alders broke the wind, but the snow was deep, coming up to his belly. He moved toward the big tree where he had tramped the snow into a hard mass. The branches of the tree would keep some of the wind from striking him. Halting under the tree, he started digging in an attempt to uncover the dead leaves under the snow.

Looking up into the tree, Charlie saw a black object moving back and forth under a big limb. It was about the size of a small squirrel, but it wasn't a squirrel. It swung lower and he saw that it was attached to a yellow tail. With a loud snort he leaped away from the tree.

The cougar had been waiting for Charlie to turn around and expose his back to a smashing blow that would break the horse's neck. Seeing that his prey was alerted, he leaped, sailing far out in a spring which would carry him at least thirty feet. The force of his descent was terrific, starting as it did from twenty feet up in the tree. He had been forced to calculate fast, like a hunter taking a snap shot at a bounding deer, but he was an expert at striking fast. His powerful claws were unsheathed and spread wide, ready to sink into Charlie's neck and twist it around.

Charlie was a straight-away runner which was bad in such a contest. His plunging body offered a fairly steady target. But one small thing was in his favor. His second leap took him under the limb of a near-by tree. There was nothing the killer could do about that limb. In his split-second calculation he had not considered the limb. His chest struck it and smashed the brittle wood, but the limb deflected his big body and he landed in the snow a yard in front of Charlie.

The big dun did not try to swerve; he hit the big cat as he was twisting around to right himself and lash out. Charlie was no fighting stallion, but he weighed twelve hundred pounds and he was still wearing the iron shoes he had been fitted with before he took to the wild. He was simply a terrified horse who wanted to get into the open where he could use the defense he knew best, his speed. The shod hoofs bowled the cougar over on his back, and Charlie charged over him and galloped on to open ground.

The cougar gathered himself together. Snarling savagely, he limped to the edge of the grove where he lay down. He was badly shaken but not seriously injured, and he had not given up his intention of pulling down the horse. He would have to find another way to make his kill. His yellow eyes flamed as he raised his head and stared down across the meadow.

Charlie did not lie down that night and he did not seek shelter beside a thicket or under a tree. He turned his back to the biting wind and lowered his head, but he remained watchful. A pale half moon lighted the open meadow, but there were pools of black shadow back of every bush, thicket, and rock. Charlie watched the shadows, looking for movement. The wind prevented his hearing anything, but he listened anyway.

Because he was in the open and not hidden inside the grove, the old she-wolf and her three sons spotted him toward midnight. They had left the elk yard after three days of fruitless watching. The remaining elk were all in good condition and they had long since become aware of the wolves. It was a case of hunt elsewhere or starve. It was the old she-wolf who caught Charlie's scent as they loped past the spot where he stood. She gave a low eager snarl which her sons recognized as a signal that game had been sighted. When she swerved upward they leaped along beside her. The deep snow made their pace slow compared to the usual speed of their attack. They plunged through the storm like gray shadows and when they sighted Charlie they sounded the cry of the kill, a savage chorus that swirled downwind and roused the big cougar to a frenzy of anger. In true wolf fashion they fanned out so as to strike from several angles, a tactic calculated to allow one of them to hamstring their victim and deprive him of the use of a hind leg.

Charlie had never before faced a pack of wolves, but he sensed that in this case he needed cover. He lunged toward a dense clump of scrub oak. If he got past it, he might outrun the killers. But they were snapping on his heels when he swerved to dash around the thicket. The teeth of the she-wolf ripped skin from one leg, missing the tendon by inches. Charlie pivoted and pushed his rump against the tangle of scrub oak. His hoofs flailed out, sending the she-wolf tumbling over and over in the snow.

The three sons leaped aside, waiting for their leader to get her feet under her. She got up slowly and shook herself. Snarling savagely, she leaped forward. The scrub oak at Charlie's back was tough as iron, its branches twisted together. No rider ever tried to push his horse through such a thicket. In desperation Charlie forced half of his body into the thicket. He lashed at the she-wolf with his shod hoofs and again sent her spinning.

The wolves did not have Charlie's weight; they could not penetrate to the scrub oak to get at his rear. One of the dog wolves tried a flank attack while another leaped at Charlie's muzzle. The gelding smashed the leaping wolf back, and lashed at the one coming in from the side. The old she-wolf dragged herself out of a snow bank. Her shoulder was so badly bruised that she stood on three legs. She growled deeply, then turned and started limping away. Her sons still wanted to make the kill. The third wolf started circling the thicket, seeking a way to get at Charlie's rear.

The she-wolf halted on high ground and watched the maneuvers. The young wolves did not leave until the sun came up, but none of them dared attempt another frontal attack. Their desperate hunger kept them close to the spot where Charlie was making his stand. But when the sun broke through the scattering clouds, they moved off and started down to visit the elk yard with their mother limping after them. The cougar watched them go but did not move out of the alder thicket inside the cottonwood grove. He would stay because this was his best chance to secure meat.

Charlie came out of the scrub after the wolves left. He was hungry and very tired. He needed food, and he had to find a place where he could rest safely. The sky was fast clearing, but there was little heat in the rays of the sun. He dug down to grass on an open slope and fed well. Toward noon he headed for the cliffs overlooking the canyon. The rimrocks were high and vertical with ledges ridging their faces. They offered fine cover for a cougar but not much protection for a horse.

A short distance below the cottonwood grove he came to an outthrust formation of rock which jutted out from the cliff wall. The hard strata had not weathered away as fast as the sandstone under it, which had formed a cave like those once used by the cliff dwellers as shelter for their stone houses. Charlie had to scramble up over a five-foot ledge to reach the small cavern, but he managed, and when he was inside he lay down facing the entrance. Here at least he would have a chance to spot an approaching enemy and make a stand.

The cougar trailed Charlie and studied his hideout from a ledge above it. The set-up was not to his

liking. He had learned that the gelding could use
his hoofs with punishing effect. There was no place
above the entrance where he could crouch to drop
upon the horse when he left the cave. But he did not
go away. He lay on the ledge and let the feeble sun
warm his lank body.

Down in the valley Black Lady was sick and weak.
The herd had stripped most of the bark and limbs
from the trees in the groves they used for shelter.
Snow fell without wind, covering the exposed grass
on the ridge. Ebony dug down for grass and fed well,
but his mother lacked the strength and spirit to dig.
She stopped fighting the wild mares for her share of
the scant browse in the groves.

Then a day came when the air softened and the
snow settled. All day long warm wind blew up from
the desert. That night the packed and softened snow
froze, forming a hard crust over the surface. Now
the wolves and the cougars could run swiftly over
the top of the snow while the horses, elk, and deer
broke through and floundered helplessly.

Up in the canyon, the big cougar stopped watching Charlie and set off for the valley where he could
now pull down mule deer. The four wolves left the
elk yard and did the same.

Black Lady and Ebony moved with the herd to
dig for grass. The going was slow and sapped her
strength. Big Baldy led them high along the ridge

seeking a spot where the grass was exposed. They traveled two miles before stopping and settling down to break the crust so they could get at the grass and shrubs underneath. Getting feed was now no easy task, it was hard slow work. Black Lady went at it halfheartedly.

Late in the afternoon Big Baldy started the herd back toward one of the groves. Black Lady stood belly deep in the crusted snow and watched them leave. Ebony was above her, keeping an eye on the big herd leader. The herd stallion paused and looked back. He stamped in the snow and whinnied a command. Black Lady did not move; she just lowered her muzzle until it rested on the crust. Big Baldy shook his head in anger, then screamed and started plunging toward the mare. Ebony backed away, but he whinnied defiantly. Already the instincts of a mature stallion were stirring in him. Big Baldy ignored the colt. He swung around the mare and nipped her flank sharply. She stumbled forward a few steps. His teeth found her rump, and he bit her savagely. Black Lady plunged and fell headlong in the snow. She did not move when Big Baldy slashed at her.

Ebony moved in closer and whinnied. Big Baldy whirled and charged the colt, his ears back, his teeth bared. Ebony was off at once, plunging wildly through the snow. The big stallion halted and screamed his anger, then turned and walked toward Black Lady. He nuzzled her flank, but he did not punish her further. After watching her a few minutes, he loped away down the ridge to catch up with the herd. Ebony moved to his mother's side. There was still a bond between them. He did not want to leave her lying in the snow.

He was standing beside her still form when Charlie appeared, attracted by Big Baldy's screams. He moved in and touched Black Lady's side with his nose. The mare did not respond. Her eyes stared unseeingly into space. Black Lady's struggle to survive was over.

Charlie stayed a while with Ebony close to him. Finally he moved off to return to his cave. He had located the grove where the herd stayed and was satisfied that later on he could find the horses. Ebony looked around uneasily. Something warned him that he should get back to the safety of the herd. With a low nicker he started off.

A pair of coyotes sat on a drift a hundred yards above the spot where Black Lady lay. A short distance below them a fox thrust his head out of a thicket. They all knew that here was a feast better than the leavings from a cougar kill. As soon as Ebony was well away from the carcass, they moved in.

Ebony was not really lonely any more. For a

while he missed his mother, but the ties between them had become weak. He stayed with the herd, and he kept away from the scarred gray stallion. Two colts and one of the branded mares had died of weakness caused by hunger. All of the horses were gaunt, their ribs forming ridges under their shaggy hides, but they were alive and would survive.

At last a real chinook came, a warm wind out of the south. The snow settled and rivulets of water ran in every ravine and arroyo. The warm wind carried the smell of plants already sprouting on the desert below. It aroused uneasiness in the herd, but Big Baldy wasn't ready to drive them into the lower country. The snow was still deep and the crust thicker than before. It amounted to a layer of ice which required heavy blows to break through to grass. The horses sought willow patches and browsed on the stems. The cottonwood groves had been stripped of anything the mares could reach.

But the day finally came when patches of bare earth showed and dead grass was exposed. The smells from below were stronger and filled the mares with an urge to go seeking new grass. The coyotes and the wolves began to run in pairs under the stars, and the nights were filled with their love calls.

Charlie moved down from his cave and stayed close to the herd. Now that the mating moon had arrived Big Baldy hated the gelding more than ever. He was savagely jealous of the old race horse. But

Charlie had lost none of his speed. He seemed to get a lot of satisfaction out of baiting the big gray. Ebony often joined Charlie. He was the only horse in the herd who was friendly to him. The growing colts ignored him, while the mares bit and kicked him if he got close to them.

The day came when Big Baldy was ready to move his herd to the lower range. He started the mares off early one morning. Ebony moved along with the herd between himself and the stallion. Charlie loped along above the mares. Ebony did not know that the leader had singled him out as a colt who had to be disposed of. The other youngsters were mares, so Big Baldy did not bother them. Toward evening that day the herd reached a mesa which was free of snow.

Now the herd stallion was ready to act. There was plenty of open, almost level prairie which made an attack upon the youngster easy. The mesa broke off sharply at its lower end in a steep drop of more than a hundred feet, but there was room to maneuver on top. Big Baldy lost no time in making his attack. As soon as the mares started pulling the short new grass, he charged Ebony with his teeth bared. Ebony fled but he screamed as defiantly as he could. It was more of a squeal than a scream. He raced away across the mesa with Big Baldy pounding after him. Ebony fled toward the lower end of the mesa which was a mistake. When it was too late to do anything about it, he realized that Big Baldy had him trapped with no place to go but over the rim and down the almost vertical drop off, just what the big stallion wanted.

Ebony whirled to meet the charge of the veteran. In that instant he became a stallion ready to do battle. But he knew nothing about fighting. Big Baldy reared and lashed at him with teeth and hoofs. Ebony leaped aside and backed a few steps toward the rim. Big Baldy lunged again, his teeth ripping at the colt's neck, his big hoofs pounding. Ebony had his forefeet working, but not effectively. The veteran outweighed Ebony by at least six hundred pounds. The colt reeled backward under the blows rained upon him and teetered on the edge of the drop off. Big Baldy pressed his advantage and Ebony was pounded back another step. Then he was falling, lunging and kicking, trying to steady himself on the almost vertical slope. He plunged down the steep bank, sliding and skidding until he went down and shot forward on his side. Halfway down, a big clump of sage broke his speed, but it was uprooted, letting him shoot on down to the bottom. When he struck the bottom he was so stunned that he lay still.

Up on the rim Big Baldy sent a triumphant scream ringing over the mesa before he whirled and galloped back to his harem. He was sure he had rid himself of a potential rival. The mares had watched the fight at its start, but had returned to their grazing before it was over. Now they watched the big stallion as he galloped toward them. They were uneasy because it was clear he was in one of his rages.

At the bottom of the cliff, Ebony finally got to his feet. He was battered and had lost some skin, but no bones were broken. He began looking for a way to climb back to the mesa. It took an hour, but he finally found a ravine leading upward. When he reached the top, he whinnied and looked around. He did not see the herd, but his call was answered from far below. He started off at a lope.

A half hour later he came upon Charlie. The gelding was standing on a rim looking down upon another mesa. He nickered to Ebony, and the young stallion moved in close beside him. On the mesa below, the herd was feeding peacefully. The sight of Big Baldy standing guard over the mares stirred anger in Ebony. He lifted his head and whinnied loudly. Charlie started to climb down to be near the herd. Ebony went with him.

In the days which followed, the young stallion, taught by Charlie, learned how to evade the attacks from Big Baldy. Charlie was never trapped on the rim of a mesa. Ebony quickly learned that he could outrun the big gray, outdodge him, and need not stand to fight. Now Big Baldy had two followers of his herd to rouse his wrath. They kept him in a constant rage.

Ebony had as yet felt no urge to have a harem of

his own, but he was developing fast, and one day he would be seeking mares of his own. It was the herd instinct which made him want to stay close to Big Baldy's mares. He was glad to have Charlie's companionship, and Charlie was happy to have the young stallion with him. They were never far apart. With two of them to keep an eye on Big Baldy, there was no danger of a surprise attack.

The Tall Grass Calls

LIFE on the dry mesas below the foothills was not very rewarding. The mares spent all of their time searching for scattered patches of bunch grass. The grass was short and the bunches small. Ebony and Charlie fared better than the mares. They could roam as they wished while the mares were kept together by Big Baldy. With the passing of the time when rain fell, the desert began to dry up.

The sand storms which blew in from the flat country below the mesas were worse in many ways than the winter blizzards had been. The first one that struck sent Charlie into a deep canyon with Ebony at his heels. Blasts of hot wind swirled fine sand into the air in clouds which enveloped the rims, arroyos,

85

and mesas. The air was dense with choking particles of sand. Down in the canyon the pair found shelter on the lee side of a cliff where they stood with lowered heads and waited out the storm.

Big Baldy drove his herd into a deep arroyo. He did not trust desert canyons; too many of them were box canyons where a herd could be trapped by wandering Navajo Indians who were always on the lookout for wild horses to add to their herds.

When the storm blew itself out, the mares were thirsty and hungry and so were Charlie and Ebony. Charlie headed for a waterhole he had located a few days before the storm hit. Ebony moved along beside him. They reached a rocky depression filled with brackish water and had just started to drink when Big Baldy appeared with his herd. The mares shoved in eagerly and began drinking. Ebony and Charlie were in the midst of a shoving mass of mares, all so eager for water that they paid no attention to the gelding and the young stallion.

Not so with Big Baldy; in a rage he charged down upon the waterhole, screaming loudly. Thirsty as they were, the mares scattered. Charlie was off at once, bowling over a young mare as he bolted for open ground. Big Baldy sent a mare staggering out of his path and charged at Ebony. Ebony lacked the weight to bowl over any of the mares or to shoulder them aside. He ducked and dodged in an attempt to get into the clear where he had running room and he got in the only blow struck in the contest. He lashed out with his heels and caught Big Baldy on his muzzle. The gray screamed and reared up, giving Ebony enough time to duck past a mare and reach open ground. Once in the clear, he sped away with the old stallion pounding after him. Big Baldy didn't continue the chase long. Ebony quickly ran away from him. The leader soon turned back to the waterhole.

Charlie watched the chase from a sand dune. When the stallion turned and started back to his herd, he whinnied to Ebony. Ebony answered him and galloped over to join him on the dune. They were both thirsty as they had had time to drink only a little water. They watched the horses at the waterhole. The mares took their time and so did Big Baldy. They knew it was not wise to drink a lot of water fast. Foundering could be as bad as colic from eating poison weed. Finally the mares moved away from the water. Big Baldy stood beside the hole, looking up the slope at the pair on the dune, and when he left the water he did not move far. He didn't want to let the two he hated get a drink. When he returned to his herd he held the mares close enough to the waterhole so that he could guard it.

Ebony and Charlie finally left the dune and started searching for grass. Ebony went close to a sage clump where bunch grass was growing. His lip twitched as he took a mouthful. He was about to pull another mouthful when a sidewinder slithered out of the sage clump. The rattlesnake seemed to be moving sidewise. It made a ladderlike, zigzag track in the sand. Ebony snorted loudly. He knew nothing about sidewinders and was curious. When he lowered his muzzle toward the snake it instantly coiled and raised its diamond-shaped head. Its tail quivered and it rattled loudly.

Charlie was feeding near-by. At the sound of the rattles he jerked up his head and whinnied a sharp warning. Ebony stamped one foot, and the rattler struck. Its fangs grazed Ebony's nose as he jumped back. Charlie whinnied again and started off. Having been bitten by one when he was a colt, he knew about rattlers, and always put a safe distance between himself and a snake. Ebony trotted after him but soon halted to look back just in time to see a strange-looking bird with a long neck and a sharp beak dart out of a cactus patch.

The roadrunner was long-legged and ran rather than flew toward the coiled sidewinder. The ungainly bird struck at the snake with its big feet, stamping furiously. Its slender beak darted out and jerked the snake upward, neatly uncoiling it. The roadrunner was as big as a prairie hawk, and it had powerful legs because most of its traveling was done on foot. It stamped the snake and tore at it with its beak. In a few minutes the fight was over and the roadrunner was dining on snake meat.

Ebony and Charlie went on feeding, keeping one eye on the waterhole, the other on Big Baldy. The mares were drifting slowly southward, but the stallion was slow to follow them. Finally Ebony decided that the big fellow was far enough away from the waterhole to allow him to get a drink. He edged toward the water, but Big Baldy saw what he was doing and screamed loudly, then charged down the slope. Ebony was able to snatch only one swallow of water before he had to leap away. He dashed off across the mesa with the stallion after him. Charlie saw his chance and slipped down to the pond and drank deeply. When Big Baldy saw Charlie at the waterhole he pulled up, and with an angry scream charged back to drive the gelding away from the water. Charlie fled, but he did not try to keep far ahead of the stallion; he had drunk a lot of water and did not feel like putting on extra effort.

Now it was Ebony's turn. He ran to the hole and drank. Big Baldy chased Charlie a half mile before he gave up. Having the gelding almost within reach spurred him on. Winded at last, he pulled up. His herd was scattering and beginning to move fast. Big Baldy gave up the contest and loped away to round up his mares.

There wasn't anything to keep Charlie and the colt from leaving the desert, but they were herd animals and felt more secure when near other horses. Charlie often stood on a ridge looking north toward where the Crazy Kill Mountains stood blue against the spring sky, but he never started off on the long trek back to the tall grass country.

Finally, Big Baldy headed his mares north. The distant mountains stirred the mares with eager excitement. They grazed but they kept on the move and Ebony and Charlie moved with them. One afternoon they reached rocky foothills of cedar and piñon timber with large bunches of sage brush growing on the slopes. There was now some browse as well as better grass.

It was in this rough country that Big Baldy showed a trait that was probably inborn. He never went around a barrier if he could jump over it. Few horses are born jumpers; most who turn out to be jumpers have been taught to clear high barriers. In the hands of a good trainer, Big Baldy might well have become a champion. He leaped over fallen trees and sandstone barriers. He seemed to feel that all horses should jump and often sent his mares charging at a barrier. This had brought disaster to some of his mares, but that did not matter. The mares he now had with him could all jump. The weaklings had long since been weeded out by injuries.

Ebony first learned about Big Baldy's jumping ability one day when he was resting in a spot that seemed safe from the stallion. It was an outcrop of sandstone about five feet high which ran along a slope for about a mile. Ebony had located a break in it and had trotted along the outcrop for some distance before he stood to enjoy the shade.

While circling his herd, Big Baldy spotted the colt enjoying a shady spot close to the wall. He sounded off and galloped forward. Ebony did not move, feeling quite safe with a five-foot barrier between himself and the stallion. But Big Baldy did not turn aside when he reached the outcrop; he tucked in his forefeet and with a mighty thrust from his hind legs, he went up and over the wall like a show horse. Ebony was so startled that he almost failed to get away. Big Baldy was on him before he could leap aside. But the big stallion only got to bite Ebony's rump once. The pain made the colt move faster than he had ever run before. He fled down along the wall and ducked through the break. Out on the slope he wheeled about to look for Big Baldy. He had been in a tight spot; there was a rimrock just beyond the wall which he could not have climbed.

Big Baldy disdained the break in the wall. He circled and sailed over the barrier, then started after Ebony again. But now the colt was in the open. He raced away and soon the stallion had to give up the chase.

Several days later when Ebony was racing with Charlie, they came to a fallen tree which rested on broken limbs some three feet above the ground. Charlie dodged around the tree, but Ebony sailed over it. He was so pleased with himself that he circled and jumped over the barrier a second time. Charlie did not approve; he could see no sense in leaping over something he could duck around.

It was the middle of May before the herd reached the safety of the breaks in the high country. They were sighted by Tex, Major Howard's foreman, but Tex was alone and did not try to shoot the scarred old stallion or scatter his herd. His orders were to destroy any wild horses he sighted, but Tex wasn't the sort to shoot any kind of a horse unless he was forced to do it. He rather admired the big gray for being able to take care of himself and his herd.

The country they passed through was familiar to the remaining branded mares, who had been stolen from ranches in the vincinity. They were able to get away from Big Baldy in a heavy thunderstorm, and he could not overtake them and bring them back into his herd. They drifted down to their home ranches. Now his harem was down to eight mares. Winter and accidents had taken a toll, and Big

Baldy was not an easy master. When he stampeded the herd, he did not worry about life or limb. But his way worked well because it eliminated the weak mares who would slow down the whole herd when speed and strength meant escape.

Having such a small herd worried him. He held the mares in the breaks for a week, then headed his herd down toward the range where Major Howard kept his fine mares under the protection of Ebony's father. Ebony and Charlie went along out of habit.

The herd came to Major Howard's horse pasture. The high pole fence was not a barrier to Big Baldy, but it proved to be too much for his mares. When he sent them at it they refused the jump, swinging right and left along the fence. But Big Baldy had sighted mares, a fine herd of twenty, feeding in a meadow below the fence. The big stallion did not know it, but here was a prize—a herd of mares with long blood lines, all carefully selected by the major. To Big Baldy they were just mares.

He galloped to the fence, set himself, and went up and over. What he had not noticed was that the herd was guarded by a big black stallion. Midnight was a match for any wild stallion. When he saw Big Baldy coming, he screamed and charged to meet him. Big Baldy screamed back. He was willing to fight for the mares he wanted. They crashed together with hoofs flailing and teeth ripping. The impact set Big Baldy back on his heels. Midnight was tough and solid. He had fought other stallions when he was a wild horse. He was on Big Baldy the instant the big gray staggered back. Big Baldy knew he had met a horse he could not batter into submission. He couldn't outrun Midnight, but he had to retreat. He charged away toward the fence with Midnight ripping at his flanks. When he came to the barrier he went up and over, but he was so harassed that he banged his hind hoofs on the top rail.

Midnight was startled to see the intruder make such a jump. He slid to a halt and screamed loudly; then he charged up and down along the fence, watching Big Baldy drive away his herd.

Ebony stood at the edge of an aspen grove and watched his father. Charlie had retreated into the depths of the grove when the battle started. He was afraid of the big black stallion. Ebony knew the big fellow was dangerous; any horse that could put the run on Big Baldy was to be feared. And yet he was curious. Finally he trotted off after Charlie, who was following the wild herd.

Big Baldy did not travel far from the Bar T horse pasture. He couldn't give up the idea of trying to steal some of those mares. He would not be so bold next time, but he might be able to get away with a few of the black stallion's mares.

One of the major's riders saw the stallion and his

herd. They were too small a herd to cause much concern, but he had his order to get rid of the wild horses. He spent most of one afternoon trying to get into a position where he could get a shot at the big stallion. He learned a lot about the crafty ways of a wild horse.

He finally got his chance. He had tied the mare he was riding in a grove and was hunting on foot because the mare might give him away by sounding off when she smelled the wild horses. He crept close to a meadow where Big Baldy was letting his mares graze, but as the big stallion never let them feed in the open except in the evening or at night the light was very poor. His bullet merely creased Big Baldy's neck. The scarred veteran sounded the stampede call and the herd thundered away. Ebony and Charlie fled with them. Ebony did not know what the shooting meant. Charlie knew about guns, but did not fear them. Riders had shot from his back often. He raced along because he didn't want to be left behind.

Big Baldy knew what the shot meant. It added another scar to three he carried as reminders of what men with rifles did to wild horses. He drove his herd back up into the safety of the high broken country where Old Clubfoot was king and where the old tom cougar ranged.

Ebony met the old bear again on a sunny morning

as he was grazing well above the herd near the aspen grove the king used for tree marking. A mare had slipped away to drop her foal in a thicket close to the aspen grove. Ebony was curious, but when he approached the thicket she drove him away. Charlie was also interested, but he was wise enough not to try to make friends with the newly born foal. The mare left her baby bedded down while she fed below the thicket. Within a few hours the little filly would be able to run at her side. Wild colts have to get their legs working quickly if they are to survive.

The old bear came out of the grove and saw Ebony. He was in a surly mood; the war with the now almost-grown brothers was on again. He had chased the brown bear that morning before entering the grove. Ebony looked like a grown horse to him and he did not want to tackle so big an animal. But he was interested in what had attracted Ebony to the thicket. His bear curiosity was somewhat dulled, but it was still in him. He ambled down toward the thicket, grunting sourly.

Ebony galloped away and stood on high ground, watching. The old bear moved into the thicket swinging his massive head from side to side, his little eyes probing. Pushing aside a few branches, he saw the helpless colt. He moved in and seized it by the loose skin of its back. Swinging it clear of the bushes, he turned to retreat. He knew that its mother might be near-by and he wanted to make off to a spot where he could dine unmolested. The colt called wildly for its mother and kicked with its small legs.

The call brought an instant answer from the mother. She whinnied wildly as she dashed up the hill. It also alerted Big Baldy, who was on guard below. He came pounding up the slope. The big bear was not a speedy runner, and he was carrying a dangling colt. One look back convinced him that if he was to escape unscathed, he'd have to drop his prize. He dropped the little horse and swerved downhill. Big Baldy was hot on his heels. Clubfoot smashed through underbrush and over saplings, going around only the bigger trees. He didn't stop to climb a tree; he knew that the stallion's teeth would rake his rump before he could get out of reach. Big Baldy halted when he was sure he had routed the enemy. He screamed after the charging bear.

Ebony watched and a feeling of rage against the bear made him scream almost as loudly as Big Baldy. He stamped about and pawed the ground. This brought Big Baldy's wrath down upon him. The old stallion chased Ebony up into the aspen grove. He did not appreciate the support Ebony was giving him. He didn't need any assistance in attacking a bear.

The summer passed and winter came again.

Ebony was growing big and strong. Charlie could no longer run away from him. And he was beginning to feel the urges of a stallion, the urge to stand his ground and fight when Big Baldy chased him, the urge to roam though he had no idea what he was seeking. Winter had temporarily stilled these stirrings. The battle to survive the blizzards and the cold kept him busy. Again it was food and shelter that counted. But he came through strong and healthy and bigger.

Fence Buster

Big Baldy's herd was down to five mares and two yearling fillies when spring came. The herd had wintered in the high country above the Bar T range. There had been no long trek to the desert that spring. Ebony and Charlie had stayed close to the mares in spite of the old stallion's hostility. Staying in the high country through the early spring meant living on last year's grass for an extra month.

Big Baldy had to find wild mares or raid a ranch. He could not be satisfied with so small a harem. It was Ebony who helped him, and also a turn of events down at the Bar T ranch.

About the time the first leaves appeared on the willows and aspens, Ebony became restless. Charlie wasn't stirred by an urge to roam; he had serious business to attend to—the business of regaining the fat and flesh he had lost during the winter. So Ebony set off alone and headed up country.

Ebony moved up through the rough breaks toward the mountains. He climbed over a ridge and wandered down into Lazy Y range where he found grassy parks and good water. Then he turned toward the mountains and started to climb again. He did not know what he was seeking, but he had to keep moving. High up, just below the timber line, he came upon a mother bear with two cubs. She was feeding on the carcass of a horse. The horse had been a scrub stallion who had collected a herd of ten mares down on the desert. He had driven his harem up into the mountains and had invaded the Lazy Y range, which brought the wrath of the Lazy Y down upon him.

The little stallion had not been very wise. He lacked the experience needed to cope with riders armed with rifles. He had almost gotten his harem over the pass to safety, but he made the mistake of making a daylight run for it and a bullet ended his career.

Ebony halted to watch the mother bear. She would not tolerate even the presence of a horse near her cubs. When Ebony moved closer for a better look, she roared and slapped her cubs, sending them up a sapling. Then she charged the stallion. Ebony raced away with the angry bear after him. She was not old and stiff-jointed like the king bear; she was young and strong. Ebony had to put on a burst of speed to get away from her. He flashed through a stand of spruce and came out in a small park. He was surprised to see horses scattered over the meadow, feeding. Nickering eagerly, he galloped toward them.

As he galloped across the grass he called loudly. He had never screamed in such a situation before, and he did not know why he was attracted to the mares. They lifted their heads and instinctively started to bunch together. They were all wild mares and had learned to obey the commands of a stallion. They had been without leadership since the death of the young stallion killed by the Lazy Y cowboy.

Ebony circled around them, not knowing just what to do but filled with a wild desire to run. He charged toward them and screamed again. His voice lacked timbre, but it was certainly the commanding call of a herd stallion. The mares started off at a gallop down country. Ebony dropped in behind them and raced along, whinnying exultantly. He lacked a lot in matters of leading, but to the mares he was boss. He wasn't driving them any place; in fact, an old gray mare did the leading.

The black colt enjoyed running the mares. He

kept them moving until he got hungry, then he slowed down. They immediately stopped running and started to graze. Ebony fed close to them. None of the mares tried to bolt and run away. They had been uneasy ever since the young stallion was killed and the cowboy had chased them. Now they were satisfied to have a stallion look after them.

There were eight mares, four of them with colts. The range rider had managed to shoot two of their number before they escaped into heavy timber. They were all scrubs just recovering from the rigors of a winter spent on the desert. They only desired to be allowed to graze and build up their strength. Ebony let them graze until he, himself, had filled his belly; then he wanted to run again. This time he experimented by nipping the flank of a lean sorrel mare who lagged behind when the herd started off. She lashed at him with her heels. For the first time in his life Ebony flew into a real rage. He dashed after the mare and slashed at her with his teeth. This established him as master of the herd. Now he took over completely, guiding the herd down into the breaks above the Bar T horse pasture.

In the meantime, Big Baldy, looking for mares, had driven his small harem down to the pasture fence. The mares were there in the horse pasture, but he saw no sign of the black stallion who had mauled him. He screamed a challenge but got no

answer, which encouraged him. Midnight was away
being shown at a fair in the valley. Neither Major
Howard nor Tex suspected that there was a wild
stallion in the rough country above the Bar T range.
Big Baldy had been careful to keep his mares in deep
cover during the day. Tex figured that the big gray
had left the country after being creased by a bullet.
He knew the old veteran was a very smart horse.

Big Baldy had learned that he couldn't make his
mares jump the fence, but he thought that perhaps
the ranch mares could be forced to clear the barrier.
He galloped to the fence and leaped. His timing was
bad, and his hind feet knocked down the top rail,
spilling him in the grass inside the pasture. He
lunged to his feet and galloped toward the ranch
mares. They lifted their heads and watched him as
he pounded down upon them. Midnight had trained
them in the ways of a wild leader, and when Big
Baldy screamed they began crowding together. He
circled around them and headed them toward the
fence. Some of them broke and scattered, but he
managed to gather fifteen head and send them racing toward the weak spot in the fence. Eight of the
leaders were unable to halt or turn aside when they
came to the barrier. The mares behind them, lashed
on by the teeth of Big Baldy, shoved them into the
fence. The eight mares jumped and scattered the
fence poles, leaving only a fence three feet high. The

rest of the mares scattered and galloped off down the pasture.

Big Baldy was satisfied with eight mares. He knew it was dangerous to remain where men might appear at any moment. He now had a herd of thirteen mares and two fillies. None of the mares he had stolen had colts at their sides. Major Howard had driven all of the mares with foals down to the ranch. Big Baldy had a fine herd with nothing to slow them down.

He drove the mares up into the rough country where he knew every bench, canyon, and grove. Before he reached the place where he planned to hold them he had taught the ranch mares that he was master.

On the second day Big Baldy sighted Ebony and his eight mares and four colts. Ebony was doing a bad job of tending his herd. They were scattered out, feeding in the open. Big Baldy had his mares hidden in a heavy stand of timber. He galloped down the slope and started rounding up the mares. For the second time in two days Ebony's wrath was aroused. He charged in to defend his rights. Big Baldy met him head-on. Ebony was hurled back, but he lashed out, screaming and baring his teeth. He was no match for the scarred veteran. Big Baldy smashed him back, ripping his neck and inflicting wounds which would be his first battle scars. Ebony had to break away or go down under the rain of blows. He had not reached the stature of a real leader. He ran away, and Big Baldy triumphantly herded the scrub mares and the fillies into the timber to join his harem. He now had a herd of mares he considered worthy of him.

Ebony stood on a knoll and screamed his defiance and anger. He was answered by a whinny from above as Charlie appeared at the edge of an aspen grove. Glad to see his friend, Ebony galloped up the slope and joined Charlie.

Ebony stayed close to Big Baldy's herd. He now had a real reason for hanging around; he wanted to get back the mares Big Baldy had stolen. He had tasted the pleasure of being a herd boss and liked it. Charlie stayed with him, glad to have company.

Big Baldy was more watchful than ever. He worked himself into a fury every time he saw the pair and he saw to it that none of the mares wandered far from the herd. There was a sorrel filly from the Bar T who rebelled against Big Baldy. She was trim and fleet. Major Howard had plans for her. He planned to enter her in the two-year-old class that summer. She came from racing stock and showed promise of being a winner, a money horse, he hoped. Tex had orders to bring her in very soon and start training her.

Kitten watched her chance, and every time Big Baldy relaxed his vigilance she made a break for freedom. The first two times she tried to escape he headed her back into the herd and punished her cruelly, but the third time she got clear of the other mares and outran him. She was flashing across a meadow when Ebony saw her. He raced after her eagerly. Kitten was fast, but she couldn't outrun the little black stallion. He caught up with her and raced along at her side. Charlie pounded along, bringing up the rear.

Ebony did not bite the little mare or boss her; he just ran with her and she liked him. She liked Charlie, too, and he took an interest in her. When they finally stopped circling the meadow, they grazed together. Ebony still had no intention of leaving the big herd. His luck at getting one mare to run with him made him want to steal others. He didn't mind when Charlie muzzled against the mare. He hadn't reached the point where he resented another male horse, with the exception of Big Baldy.

Big Baldy fumed and wore himself out trying to recapture the filly, but he wasn't fast enough to catch her. He couldn't even catch Charlie. The trio hung around close to the herd. They played and raced and grazed together. It was great sport to run away from the gray stallion and to hear his screams of rage.

Big Baldy had his grazing areas well picked. With just a few mares to protect, there had been few problems; cover was easy to find and escape routes were not important. His mares were all wild and fast to respond; when he sounded the alarm they had known what to do. Now he had seven Bar T mares who were completely domesticated horses. Their wild instincts had been dormant for generations. Their herd boss had been a wild stallion, but he had never been given the chance to teach the ranch mares any of his wild tricks. There was no need for much herd discipline. Man was his friend and cared for him, protecting him and his mares, feeding them when the winter storms came, shooting the predators who molested them.

The gray stallion was aware that having stolen the man-owned mares he must be doubly alert against range riders. The size of the herd made protecting them against predators more difficult. During the day he held the mares in wooded terrain where there was cover and where they were close to an escape route down which he could stampede them. The high broken country above the Bar T range offered good cover, but so large a herd needed meadows with plenty of grass. Big Baldy had overextended himself, but he was savagely determined not to lose a single mare or colt.

Ebony, Kitten, and Charlie were footloose; their only concern was keeping alert against Big Baldy. Their habit of grazing in the open during the day if they felt like it, was a source of constant irritation to the gray boss, but there was nothing he could do about it. They hung about and could be easily sighted by riders. They might lead a horseman to the herd. Charlie and Kitten had never had anything to fear from man, and Ebony knew nothing about riders or rifles.

A week passed before Tex returned Midnight to the range pasture and discovered the broken fence. As soon as he made a fast tally and found that eight mares were missing, he rode into the country above the pasture with two of his men, Ed McLarin and Hank Gilly.

It was Hank's job to ride fence and check it for breaks. He had examined the smashed fence and repaired it before the men left the pasture. He was puzzled, but the evidence was clear that the invading stallion was a fence buster.

"Think it was the old gray?" Tex asked as they jogged along.

"I'd say so," Hank answered. "Must have stampeded the herd into the fence."

"Probably smashed it first," Ed said. He grinned eagerly. He was young; this was his first year as a regular hand. "We go after him?"

"We do some scouting first," Tex answered. His blue eyes studied Ed thoughtfully. "Reckon you better ride down to the ranch and report to the major."

They pulled up on high ground and looked back

at the pasture. Midnight had moved the mares down into the lower end of the pasture. He stood on a knoll looking up toward the mountains. He seemed restless though he could hardly have known that eight of his mares were missing. Shaking his big head, he whinnied loudly.

Ed frowned. He wanted to go with Tex and Hank. "He got away with Kitten. The major will raise the roof."

Tex nodded grimly. "You better shove off. Hank and I will do some scouting. Tell the major we've headed up into the rough country above the pasture. Don't rightly know just where we'll be."

"I'd be willing to bet a month's pay that he'll get up here fast with our whole crew," Hank said.

"And all armed to the teeth," Tex said grimly. He knew that he could no longer keep the old stallion from being destroyed along with his wild mares. In stealing Kitten, he had sealed his doom.

After Ed rode off, Tex and Hank headed north and soon picked up the trail of the herd. It was easy to follow even though it was old. Tex studied it carefully as they rode along. He was surprised at the size of the herd.

"At least a week old," he called across to Hank.

"Give or take a day," Hank agreed and added, "he's some hoss. Must have better'n two dozen mares rounded up."

"Smartest wild one I ever came across," Tex said.

"Been around a long time with everybody gunning for him."

"Reckon he went too far this time," Hank said grimly.

The trail faded out before they reached the high benches. A heavy thunderstorm had swept over the slopes washing away all tracks. Now it was a matter of searching carefully, studying every meadow and park and slope. Tex knew wild horses. He did not expect to find the herd grazing in the open. If he could spot just one horse or pick up the trail of the herd again, he would be able to move in on Big Baldy.

Tex and Hank rode ridges, keeping to cover, stopping often to scan parks and benches. Tex gave close attention to meadows close to timber and to canyons, many of which slotted the slopes. Hank was also an old hand at this sort of thing. His sharp eyes missed little that was alive and moving on the benches below.

They moved steadily upward along a ridge leading to the granite towers above the timber line. There was a large portion of the wild country to be covered by the time they reached the timber line. They saw elk and deer and passed the remains of a cougar-killed doe. There was nothing left of the doe but some bones and skin. Tex studied the bones.

"Can't be any new colts in the herd," he observed. "The big cats like them better than deer."

They moved on and halted in a stand of second-growth pines at the lower end of an aspen grove. The location was ideal for wild horses.

"Hey," Hank said suddenly. He pointed toward the aspen grove. Tex looked and saw a small horse flash into the open. It was a sorrel filly and Tex recognized her. Before he could say anything a young black stallion broke cover and raced after the mare. They were followed by a dun gelding. The three horses galloped across a meadow toward the pines where the men sat.

"Kitten," Tex said softly. "Running with a stallion about her age and a gelding."

"That dun looks like the Lazy Y's Charlie," Hank said and grinned. "I ought to know, I lost a wad betting against him more times than once."

Tex didn't answer; he was watching the black stallion. "Black as ebony, a double for Midnight," he finally said. His eyes followed the black stallion, appraising him. He added thoughtfully, "Black Lady ran away just before she dropped her colt. We never found her. Remember?"

"Sure do remember." Hank nodded his head slowly. "Ebony, son of Midnight. Could be."

"There goes one wild stallion we take without putting a blemish on him," Tex said.

As the three horses neared the pines below, a big gray stallion burst from the timber. He screamed savagely as he charged down the hill toward them. Kitten wheeled and so did the black stallion and the gelding. They raced back down across the meadow with the gray pounding after them. The three pulled away from the gray stallion and he slowed down, then turned and started back up the hill toward the pines. Hank laughed.

"They're making a monkey out of him." His hand dropped to the stock of his carbine and he pulled it out of its boot.

Tex lifted a hand. "No shooting," he said. "First we check his herd. If we shoot him, we'll have trouble rounding up even the Bar T mares. Without him they'd scatter all over the mountains."

"Best chance we'll probably ever get to put an end to him." Hank's gaze was fixed on Big Baldy who had halted at the edge of the timber, watching Ebony and his friends disappear into the aspen grove. With a final angry scream, the big stallion whirled and vanished into the timber.

"He sure hates that Ebony's hide," Tex said. "Lucky for us those three don't know enough to act like wild horses." He rubbed the stubble of beard on his chin thoughtfully. "It's a funny thing, but I never heard of a stallion palling around with a gelding."

"He's young. If he's Black Lady's colt, he's only a long two-year-old." Hank slid the carbine back into its boot.

Tex and Hank tied their horses in a grove. They would not risk having their horses betray them by whinnying if they scented the herd. Hank's horse was a mare and almost sure to sound off. Also, they could move more quietly on foot.

They worked their way down through the pines, keeping to cover and stopping often to listen. A big herd of mares could be kept out of sight, but even a tough old stallion couldn't keep them from coughing or stamping their feet. They heard a horse blow loudly. The sound came from below and to their right. Then they heard the stamping of a hoof. They moved on slowly and soon spotted a mare. She was standing under a red spruce, pawing the ground impatiently. They recognized her at once as one of the Bar T mares. There wasn't a bite of grass inside the stand of lodge-pole pine and spruce. The lodge poles grew so close together that no sun ever got to the ground. The ranch mare was hungry and she had always grazed when she was hungry, not just after dark. They stood watching the mare and listening. Sounds of hoofs moving on hard ground came to them, but the timber was so dense that they could not see any other mares.

"Think I know where he'll send them into the canyon if we show ourselves," Tex said. "I'll slip around and hole up there. Give me forty-five minutes, then fire a shot. I want to have a good look at that herd." He pulled his hand gun from his belt and held it out to Hank. Tex was the only Bar T hand who carried a six-gun. He preferred it to a rifle, and could shoot it as accurately.

Hank took the six-gun and looked at his watch. "Forty-five minutes," he said.

Tex started circling to the edge of the timber,

being careful not to startle any of the mares and panic the herd. Then he moved downward to the rim of the canyon and started looking for a spot Big Baldy could use as a way into it. There seemed to be only one avenue, a rutted ravine which sloped down from the rim. Tex found a thicket and sat down to wait. He looked at his watch. Ten minutes to go.

Ten minutes later a series of shots rang out, and almost at once Big Baldy screamed, sounding the order for a stampede. Minutes later the air was filled with the ring of hoofs pounding on hard ground. The first of the mares, all lean wild horses, burst from the timber, heading for the ravine in a mad charge. They were all scrubs, but they were as active as antelope. Tex was amazed at the number of mares. He was an expert at tallying, but he couldn't count the plunging mass of mares pouring into the ravine. Ducking and leaping in a frenzy of action, they were half obscured by the dust they kicked up. He was able to check the seven ranch mares because they brought up the rear with Big Baldy lashing at their sleek hips.

As they went down the ravine they were hidden by a cloud of dust and Tex could make out only vague shapes leaping along. Big Baldy's screams urged the mares on. Then came the pounding of hoofs on the rocky floor of the canyon. The stallion was driving the mares downward. Tex stood up.

Hank came running out of the timber. He pulled up and peered into the canyon.

"Heck," he said in disgust. "Missed 'em."

"There's more than two dozen, maybe as many as thirty," Tex said.

"Quite a herd he's got for himself," Hank said. "Must keep the old boy mighty busy."

"I think we'll trap them," Tex said thoughtfully. "Let the big boy help us."

"Have to find them again. He won't bring them back here." As he spoke Kitten, Ebony, and Charlie trotted out of the aspen grove below and started upward. Tex and Hank took to cover and waited. The three horses loped to the head of the ravine and started down with Charlie in the lead. The descent was a careful, sure-footed one. Charlie didn't believe in plunging down a steep, rocky ravine.

Tex turned to Hank. "I reckon we'll find them easy," he said and grinned.

"Yeah," Hank agreed. "With those three tagging along, we won't have much trouble."

Plans

EBONY AND KITTEN did not mind letting Charlie be the leader. He had been a range horse all of his life and knew many things about foraging and finding shelter. When they reached the bed of the canyon he started off at a trot. He always worried when the herd ran off and left him. As long as he could see the mares or hear them he was content. He did not vary his pace, keeping to a ground-devouring trot.

Toward evening he halted and stood looking up toward the south rim. He had heard a mare whinnying to her colt. Ebony and Kitten had been ready to climb out of the canyon for the past hour. They wanted to get to a grass meadow. Charlie nickered and started climbing the steep canyon wall. Kitten moved in close behind him, followed by Ebony. They worked their way up to the rim above.

On top they found a large meadow with a timbered slope above it. There were no horses in the meadow. Kitten and Ebony started feeding at once, but Charlie stood listening. He knew that Big Baldy would keep the mares in the timber until darkness settled. But he knew the herd was there. He heard a mare nicker and a colt answer. He trotted out into the meadow and joined Kitten and Ebony.

A doe with her fawn at her side joined the horses, and later two cow elk appeared. One of them had a calf trailing her. They paid no attention to the horses but they were alert, browsing, then stopping to lift their heads and listen. This was the hour when danger was greatest.

Ebony caught a flash of movement in a thicket close to the timber. Instinct and budding stallion habits made him lift his head and watch the thicket. The bushes stirred and a gray form crept out into the tall grass. Ebony could not see the animal, but he knew it was a killer. It was creeping toward the doe and her fawn. Then a head appeared above the grass. The hunter was a large coyote intent upon having a meal of venison. The instinct to protect against a hunter stirred in the young stallion. With a loud whinny he dashed toward the coyote, pound-

ing down upon it with teeth bared and hoofs flashing. The coyote whirled and bounded toward the
thicket. Ebony galloped after him and smashed
down bushes as he sought to locate the enemy.

The coyote was safely hidden behind a big tree.
He peered around the trunk, his lips pulled away

from his fangs, but he did not make a sound. He knew about stallions; what puzzled him was why a stallion would protect a fawn.

The mothers out in the meadow had seen the coyote. The doe bounded away with her fawn at her side. The mother elk moved close to her calf and stood staring toward the timber. She watched for a few minutes, then started feeding again. If the hunter had been a cougar, she would have fled like the doe. One lone coyote did not bother her.

Ebony returned to the meadow. Charlie had watched with mild interest while Ebony chased the coyote. Kitten was interested, too. She had made a show of being afraid of the coyote by running a short distance, then racing in a circle around the meadow.

From cover, Big Baldy watched and anger stirred in him. It wasn't the coyote that roused his wrath, it was the black stallion and his friends. This was a perfect hideout for his herd except for the three horses out in the open. They might betray him. But he didn't try to chase them away. Already the job of protecting and holding together twenty mares was beginning to slow him down.

After darkness settled he allowed the mares to come out of the woods and graze. They were very hungry and fell to pulling grass at once. Big Baldy circled around them, alert for any mare who might wish to stray. His danger now was not from man but from predators. He grazed at intervals but never relaxed his vigilance. Having eaten their fill before dark, Ebony and his friends bedded down just inside the timber and spent a comfortable night.

In the morning the three were out on the meadow as soon as it was light. Ebony investigated a small stream which ran across the lower end of the park. It foamed over the rim of the canyon and dropped twenty feet in a misty free fall. The grass was lush along the stream. Ebony whinnied to Kitten and she joined him. Charlie moved in and drank from the creek, then splashed upstream a few yards.

As they fed, Ebony noticed the tall grass ahead of him was waving. He pricked his ears forward and stretched his neck. The grass parted and a big skunk with a wide white stripe down his back ambled into the open. His plumed tail waved behind him like a white-tipped banner. Ebony snorted but the skunk paid no attention to him. The stream bank was his right of way, and he expected any animals he met to step aside and let him pass. Ebony thrust his muzzle forward and nickered loudly. Charlie raised his head and stared at the skunk, then moved away fast. He knew about skunks the same way he knew about porcupines, from experience. Kitten saw that Charlie was afraid of the small animal, and she moved away with him.

Ebony stamped one foot. This animal was too small to be dangerous, but he didn't seem to be afraid of Ebony. When the stallion pawed again the skunk stamped his forefeet and elevated his hind end in a handstand. This was a warning jesture that every wild animal knew. If they didn't know, they soon learned. Charlie whinnied warningly. Ebony, knowing the whinny was a warning of danger, leaped aside. As he did so the skunk fired a lethal stream of musk. Ebony got a good whiff even though the musk missed him. He plunged out into the meadow shaking his head and snorting. The experience made him add skunks to the list of animals he must avoid.

Major Howard arrived at the horse pasture in the morning, as Tex had expected. But Tex was surprised when the Bar T owner rode in alone. He had expected the major to bring his whole crew and demand immediate action.

Major Howard was a hard-headed businessman. He liked fine horses and prided himself on having the best mares and the best stallion in that part of the West, and he owned the best white-faced beef cattle. His bulls were all registered Herefords, and he had no liking for scrubs or low-grade animals. He dismounted and stood with his boots spread wide apart, his gray Stetson pushed back on his head, and looked at his foreman. He expected an argument from Tex regarding the disposal of the wild horses.

"Well?" he asked gruffly.

Tex told him about the wild herd. He made it clear that the wild mares were scrub animals worth little on a horse market. He saved the best for the last. When he told the major about Kitten and Ebony, the major's eyes lighted up with interest.

"This stallion? Class? As good as Midnight?"

"I'd say as good," Tex answered.

"And he has Kitten with him?"

"Kitten and a dun gelding carrying the Lazy Y brand. Hank says he's Charlie."

"No mistake about that," Hank said.

"What's a track horse doing running wild?" the major asked sharply.

Tex smiled. "You know the Lazy Y outfit. I suppose they just turned him loose. Figure to round him up if they want to use him."

The major nodded toward a pack back of his saddle. "Fix yourself some breakfast. We'll talk while you eat."

Hank built a fire. Tex got a skillet and bacon from the pack and filled a coffeepot with water. The major lighted a cigar and puffed on it while the boys fixed their breakfast. When they sat down to eat, he poured himself a cup of coffee and joined them.

"I didn't bring a crew up here," he began. "That gray stallion has a reputation for being smart. No use having a crew idle while you locate the brute and his mares." He took a swallow of coffee and waited.

"May take a day or two to locate him," Tex said. Then he took the plunge. "I figure we can trap that herd. Save time in the long run. If we shoot that stallion, his mares will scatter all over the mountain and it will take weeks to hunt them down. The gray will help us trap them. He'll stampede them and keep them bunched."

Major Howard grunted. That was a good sign; it meant he was going to take time to consider Tex's idea. Tex had no hope of saving the scarred old stallion or his scrub mares, but at least he would not have to take part in a slaughter if the major went along with his idea.

"We won't have to take care of the stallion or his wild mares," he continued. "They can't be broken, they aren't worth anything except meat. Lately wild horses have become worth enough so that hunters go after them." Tex speared a piece of bacon and started chewing on it.

The major frowned. He had not paid much attention to the market for wild horses.

"You can call the nearest plant that processes dog food. They'll come with trucks and haul the horses away. We cut out your mares and let them have the rest." Tex wiped his mouth on his shirt sleeve. "You should get at least thirty dollars a head."

"Think you can trap them?" the major asked.

"Yes," Tex said with assurance. "Once we locate the range he uses and the route he takes when he has to move out, we can build a trap and catch him and the herd."

"Take much time? Many men?"

"A crew to build the trap and plenty of men for a one-day drive." Tex got to his feet. "We'll try to locate the herd today." He smiled at Hank. "We have one thing working for us."

"What's that?"

"Kitten, the ebony stallion, and Charlie. They stay close to the herd and they feed in the open during the day." Tex picked up his saddle blanket and shook it out.

"I'll send a crew up here with a string of pack horses." The major got to his feet. "Make a list of the tools and supplies you'll need. I'd like to see that black stallion. Handle him carefully."

"We sure will," Tex promised.

After the major left, Tex and Hank saddled up. They took a lunch with them, expecting to be out all day. They faced another night beside a campfire with only their saddle blankets to keep them warm, but they were tough outdoor men and would not mind.

They knew which canyon the herd had followed. What they had to learn was where Big Baldy had driven the mares out of the canyon. There was no grass in the rocky gorge; the stallion had to leave it to find grazing. They followed the rim of the canyon for a while, moving along at a fast pace. Then they rode up on a ridge and followed it, scanning every bench, meadow, and grove of trees.

A little before four o'clock that afternoon they sighted Ebony, Kitten, and Charlie feeding on a meadow close to the rim of the canyon. Tex pulled up and Hank reined his mare to a halt.

"This is it," Tex said.

"Reckon so," Hank agreed.

"We'll check the canyon below for a spot to build the trap," Tex said thoughtfully. "After dark we'll check that meadow. If he has the herd in that grove, they'll be out grazing tonight."

Hank nodded and they rode on down the ridge. They did not get to check the canyon that evening. Finding a way to get down into it was not easy. Tex was sure there was a route into it close to the meadow where they had seen the three horses, but that was too close to Big Baldy's hideout to be used. Tex did not want the old gray to know there were men about. They rode back up the ridge and tied their horses in a grove, then made their way down to the edge of the meadow where they had seen the three horses grazing. They moved carefully from bush to bush. Big Baldy was likely to be watching the slope. Crawling into a thicket, they seated themselves to wait for nightfall.

Dusk filled the canyon and the valley below as a blazing sunset faded. Tex and Hank watched Kitten and Ebony who were still out in the meadow with Charlie. The filly and the young stallion raced around the meadow wildly while Charlie watched. Finally he joined them in a mad race up toward the timber above the grove. They were baiting Big Baldy, but he did not come out to chase them. Finally they trotted down to the creek below for a drink.

A star winked above the Crazy Kill range. It hung below a pale slice of new moon. The shapes of boulders and bushes became shadowy outlines. More stars appeared overhead. Tex flexed a leg to work a cramp out of it. Hank wished he could smoke. He was beginning to wonder if the herd was in the grove, after all.

Then a mare nickered eagerly, and soon dark shapes moved out into the meadow. The men waited until there was enough starlight to spot Big Baldy. He made it easy by galloping to a knoll less than twenty yards from where they sat. The big stallion could not smell the men; Tex had picked a spot upwind from the meadow.

Tex did not move until Big Baldy had loped down around the herd; then he nudged Hank.

"Let's go," he said softly.

They moved carefully up the slope to where their horses were hitched and mounted. At first they rode

slowly, but when they were well out of the herd stallion's hearing they let their horses have their heads.
They wanted to get to the spring and cook a hot
supper.

Down on the meadow the mares fed eagerly. Big
Baldy kept a restless vigil. He was weary, but he
would not let himself drowse or relax. Ebony, Kitten, and Charlie bedded down for the night in a
willow thicket near the creek.

Big Baldy shook his head and lowered it to graze.
He was satisfied that he had eluded the man who
had fired the shots in the grove three miles above.
He planned to hold the mares close to this grove as
long as the grass lasted. He had only one other good
hideout left and that was more than fifteen miles
away. Not many groves had exit routes into a
canyon close by.

A Trap Is Set

TEX AND HANK explored the canyon and found what they were looking for, a spot where the canyon narrowed and the walls on each side were sheer rock faces. A camouflaged fence with a wide gate in its center could be built across from wall to wall, and a second fence could be built below it, forming a tight corral. A freight wagon and, later, heavy trucks could reach the site. Where the canyon widened out into a valley below, there were plenty of aspen trees for posts and poles. With the whole Bar T crew working they could put up the corral in two days. Working from below would keep Big Baldy from suspecting that anything was wrong. Tex figured Big Baldy would hold his herd where they were as

131

long as he wasn't alarmed. The stream which formed a falls above would furnish water for the horses while they were waiting for the trucks to come and haul them away.

Tex and Hank met the trail wagons and guided them to the valley below the mouth of the canyon where the camp was made. The crew was eager to get the corral built so they could make the big drive. Major Howard wanted to have a look at the black stallion, but Tex didn't want to risk having anyone go near Big Baldy's hideout. Tex had the men add a second gate in the lower fence which would allow the meat buyers to load from below. It could also be used when they cut out the ranch mares, Ebony, Kitten, and Charlie. Tex was sure the three loners could be driven down with the herd. It was just a matter of heading them into the stampede, and he had plenty of riders to do the job.

Up on the bench above the canyon, Big Baldy was lulled into a feeling of security because no riders showed up and everything was calm and peaceful. The only thing that upset him was the presence of Ebony and his two friends. They still roused his anger, but he was beginning to get used to having them hanging around. He no longer bothered to chase them even when they ventured close to the grove. He would smash the black stallion if and when the youngster made a bid for leadership. He still wanted Kitten in his herd and watched for a chance to capture her. But Kitten liked her freedom and her companionship with Ebony and Charlie. She made sure never to get too close to the herd.

Big Baldy always followed his instincts. If he began to feel uneasy, he moved his herd, even though he could detect no sign of danger. On the third day of his stay on the bench, he became restless. Something was disturbing his feeling of security. Perhaps it was just his habit of never staying in one place very long. He began trotting to the edge of the timber, scanning the country below and the slopes above the bench. He moved to the rim of the canyon and peered into it. He saw nothing, but still he was uneasy. That night he would drive the mares over the ridge and head them toward his third hiding place fifteen miles away. This would put him higher into the wild country, close to a pass leading over to the desert side of the range.

The sun beat hotly on the meadow. Ebony and Kitten decided to go for a gallop up the slope in the shade of a stand of pines. Charlie did not think much of the idea, but he went along. Feeling lazy after the climb, they halted near the top of the ridge under a big spreading pine. Charlie fell asleep on his feet. He twitched an ear as a fly buzzed past it. Kitten rubbed her head against Ebony's shoulder and nickered softly.

Ebony's head came up and he stared at the crest of the ridge above them. He had heard the faint click of a horse's hoofs. Then he swung his head around and looked down at the grove above the bench where a rider moved quickly from one clump of pines to another. The rider interested him, but did not alarm him.

Five minutes passed. Kitten was drowsing, and Ebony had lowered his head. He was aroused by the crack of a rifle, followed by wild shouting from below. The sounds came from the upper end of the grove on the bench. Almost at once Big Baldy's scream rang out, and the distant thunder of pounding hoofs. Charlie shook himself and turned around quickly. Kitten moved closer to Ebony. She was not frightened, just startled.

The three stood looking down as Big Baldy's mares burst from the timber and headed toward the canyon rim with the big stallion lashing at the slower ones. The fleet wild mares were in the lead with the Bar T ranch mares bringing up the rear and taking punishment from the gray's teeth. The herd plunged over the rim and vanished into the canyon in a cloud of yellow dust.

The three horses did not move. They stood and watched riders appear on the canyon rim where they pulled up and looked down before sending their mounts over the rim. They had stopped shooting and yelling.

Tex was leading the drive. He let his big roan take his time descending the ravine after the wild horses. Major Howard followed him down with the rest of the Bar T crew stringing along. They did not have to take chances. But once at the bottom they sent their horses galloping down over the rocky floor. Tex wanted to keep pressure on the fleeing herd. The charging mares had raised such a dust that he could not tell whether the black stallion and Kitten were with them. He had given orders that the three loners were to be headed down to the grove, but he hadn't had time to check with his men.

Ebony moved cautiously down the slope, followed by Kitten and Charlie. He trotted to the rim of the canyon and looked down into it. A cloud of dust marked the course of the fleeing herd. Charlie nickered warningly. Seeing cowboys driving a herd of horses was nothing new to him, but he had no intention of entering the canyon. He did not want to be rounded up and driven back to the Lazy Y ranch; he liked the freedom of his new way of life. However, he did not like being parted from the herd. There was a way of keeping in touch with the mares and not being caught by the cowboys. He started off down the canyon rim. Ebony and Kitten trotted after him. They were not disturbed because the herd had darted away. It had happened a number of times before, and Charlie had always found it again.

Charlie, Ebony, and Kitten trotted along for better than a mile before they sighted the mares. The herd was no longer running. The mares were crowded together on the bed of the canyon, milling about frantically. Big Baldy was charging about, lashing at the poles of a corral fence with his big hoofs, tearing down limbs and branches which had been used to hide the fence. A dozen saddled horses stood above the corral. As many men stood outside the corral looking at the horses. Charlie knew instantly that he had been wise to stay out of the canyon.

Down at the corral, Major Howard scowled at the milling mares. "Cut out the branded stuff and start them up to the pasture," he ordered.

"Kitten and the black stallion aren't with them," Hank said. "Guess we have some hunting to do."

"Be easy to find them." Tex was watching Big Baldy and feeling sorry for the scarred veteran whose days were now numbered.

"Take it easy," the major warned. "I don't want those mares of mine injured.

His warning wasn't needed. The men knew that cutting out the ranch mares would be ticklish business with the infuriated gray stallion charging about, smashing anything he met.

"We could shoot that old brute," one of the men suggested.

"No," Tex said firmly. "He's big and in good

shape. He'll bring at least fifty dollars as meat. Dead and bloated he wouldn't be worth a dime."

Hank and Tex did the cutting out while the rest of the men mounted the fence to keep Big Baldy from bolting when the lower gate was opened. They shook out their ropes and swung them over their heads. Major Howard sat on the fence with a rifle across his lap ready to drop the big stallion if he attacked Tex and Hank when they entered the corral on foot.

The two men slipped into the corral and moved slowly toward the mares who were packed against the upper wall of the corral. The wild mares snorted and stamped, Big Baldy turned and faced the approaching men. Major Howard eased his rifle to his shoulder. But Big Baldy did not charge. He knew the men who had trapped him had guns.

"I'll take the sorrel," Tex said as he swung his rope. His loop dropped over the head of a sorrel mare. When he tightened the rope she moved forward without fighting it. She had been roped many times before. And she was weary after the mad stampede down the canyon.

Hank roped a gray mare. They led the horses to the gate. Within a half hour the seven Bar T mares and one other branded mare had been taken from the corral. The gate was lashed shut. The drive was over.

All of the men except Tex and Hank left with the

ranch mares. They were left behind to scout the country above for the three they had not caught in the trap. Big Baldy paced about and watched the men ride away. His rage had subsided and he was again the cunning old leader who had outwitted men for years.

"Kind of hate to think of those critters being hauled off to a slaughterhouse," Tex said as he and Hank sat in their saddles watching the trapped herd.

"Not one of them worth breaking." Hank was looking at one of the colts, a long-legged little mare. "Might be able to do something with the colts but not the others."

"Yeah," Tex agreed. He was watching the old stallion. The scarred veteran ·was hammerheaded, and no foal of his would have class. But the horses he had fathered had all been tough and able to take care of themselves, and the big fellow had always been a leader who had been free. Anyway, his end would come quickly; the meat processors wouldn't keep him around a day longer than they had to, and he'd go down fighting. His spirit would never be broken, Tex was sure of that.

They rode down the canyon to the camp where the men had left supplies for a couple of days. They would start looking for the black stallion and Kitten the next morning.

Ebony and Kitten were grazing close to the canyon rim. Charlie stood looking down into the corral. He wouldn't go down to it, but he was uneasy about the mares penned up below. He had escaped from fences and meant to stay clear of them.

Down in the corral, Big Baldy's rage had changed to hatred. His old shrewdness had returned and a measure of hope came to him. He had to find a way to free his mares from the corral. He looked at the upper barrier. The fence was higher than any barrier he had ever jumped; Tex had insisted on putting an extra row of poles on it. The men had grumbled; not even a trained jumper could leap over a six-foot fence, much less seven feet, they argued. Big Baldy would be a world champion if he leaped over that fence, Ed said.

Big Baldy circled to the lower gate then whirled and ran toward the upper fence. He swung along with powerful strides, pacing himself carefully. As he came to the barrier he gathered himself together, tucked in his forelegs and thrust powerfully with his hind legs. His forefeet cleared the barrier, but his hind quarters hit the top pole. His great weight sent the pole flying as he went over. He landed on his knees outside the corral, his muzzle plowing a furrow in the dirt. Lunging to his feet, he whinnied loudly to his mares. They did not move, so he lunged recklessly at the fence and leaped. This was no careful jump, it was badly timed; he was too far from

the barrier to clear it. His body smashed into the
fence. The green poles had been spiked to the inside
of the posts. No attack from the outside had been
expected. Poles flew under his weight and scattered
on the ground. The fence was now only three feet
high.

Inside the corral Big Baldy lashed at the mares,
forcing them to charge the low barrier. Some of
them went over and their bad jumping knocked
down more poles. In less than a half hour Big Baldy
had freed his herd. He lost no time in driving them
down the canyon to a point where they could climb
out. He lost only one horse, a colt that was trampled
when the herd charged the fence.

Up on the rim Charlie watched the escape and
whinnied eagerly. He started off along the rim still
whinnying excitedly. Ebony and Kitten followed
him. Now that the herd was free Charlie wanted to
go along with them.

They met the herd moving up country. Big Baldy
was pushing the mares hard, having decided that
the high country was no longer a safe place. He was
in too big a hurry to waste time on the three hangers-
on. He wanted to put miles between himself and
the trap. Down on the desert there were canyons to
hide in and mesas from which he could watch the
surrounding country and spot riders when they were
miles away. The grass would not be tall and lush

and the waterholes would be far apart, but the dry wasteland would be safer than the mountains.

Once over the pass, Big Baldy let his herd halt and graze. He did not seek cover but let the mares feed on an open slope. If riders showed up, he would stampede the mares into the foothills below.

Ebony didn't understand why the gray stallion was in such a hurry. He had never known the stallion to run his mares so far without letting them blow and feed. The miles they had covered had not taken his strength or that of Kitten, but Charlie was weary and glad to halt and rest. Ebony looked around for water and found a trickle seeping out of a bank. He followed the trickle and found a pool where he could drink. Kitten and Charlie joined him, and they took turns drinking, draining the pool and waiting for it to refill. Big Baldy did not worry about water; he knew that there was a stream a mile below. He started the weary mares off, snapping at them savagely, forcing them to gallop. His escape had filled him with a new strength. He had met another challenge and had won a victory.

A Price on His Head

Tex and Hank learned of Big Baldy's escape late in the afternoon of the second day of hunting for Ebony and Kitten. They had been unable to find any trace of the black stallion and his companions and had returned to the canyon rim thinking the three might be near the corral where the mares were penned up. When Tex looked down at the empty corral he smiled grimly.

"The old boy is smarter than we thought," he said.

"The major will have a fit," Hank said anxiously. "We better ride in and report."

"No use looking for that ebony horse"—Tex touched his horse's flank with a spur—"the major will really blister me for this."

Major Howard was furious when Tex told him about the escape. The matter became a personal contest between himself and the gray stallion. He posted a reward of a hundred dollars for Big Baldy's capture. His men tacked up the reward signs on trees as far south as the Navajo reservation on the New Mexico desert. Tex had an idea the stallion might drive his herd south into the desert, and also thought the big fellow would come back to the high country after a time. Major Howard was sure he'd be back and start raiding again.

When the Navajo heard of the reward they started looking for Big Baldy and his harem. They were nomads who covered a lot of territory grazing their herds of sheep, always moving because there was little grass. They lived in summer hogans which were no more than racks of poles with brush on top to furnish shade. During the day the men and boys rode out over the desert hunting and gathering small bundles of sticks for cooking fires.

Tribal customs among the Navajo decreed that the children, the sheep, and the hogans belonged to the women. The men owned the horses, war implements, and turquoise jewlery. A man's wealth was judged by the number of horses he owned. The reward for the capture of Big Baldy was attractive, but the chance to add mares to their herds was an even bigger lure. Among the Navajo, even the boys

were experts in capturing and taming horses. They
had their own methods.

It was a pair of Navajo boys who first sighted the
herd. They were out prairie-dog hunting and had
stopped at a waterhole for a drink. They noticed
horse tracks at the waterhole and followed the trail
which led into a canyon. They were wildly excited
when they saw the stallion and his big herd of mares.
They ran the two miles to their hogan and reported
to their father.

Tall Man knew that he and his sons could not
capture the stallion and his mares alone. Word was
sent to other scattered camps and a big meeting was
held. Careful plans were made for a wild-horse
drive. Tall Man and his friends scouted the canyons
where the herd had been seen. The horses were
there, as the boys had said.

The Navajo plan was simple and much more
effective than Tex's trap. These men knew every
watering place in the desert and every canyon and
mesa. They scattered out over the wasteland in
small groups, most of them mounted but a few on
foot. Parties of three or four, mostly boys, camped
at the waterholes. The riders scattered out over the
desert. Tall Man and his sons rode to the canyon
where Big Baldy held his mares during the day.

Ebony, Kitten, and Charlie were on a mesa above
the canyon when Tall Man and his sons entered it

to drive the herd out to open country. The three
loners never entered the canyon because it was difficult to elude the big stallion in the narrow gorge.
Tall Man made no effort to catch any of the horses;
he simply flushed them out of their hiding place.

Big Baldy sent his mares charging up a side ravine
and out on the mesa above. He drove them in a
great circle which would bring them back to the
canyon hideout. Tall Man knew what would happen
and did not follow the herd. He and his sons,
Benji and Little Tom Crow, sat in the shade of a
ledge and waited.

Twice during the circling the herd was sighted by
riders and chased for a few miles. The mares tired
after hours of running in the hot sun. Their lungs
were choked with dust and they were thirsty. Big
Baldy headed them toward a waterhole, but as they
approached it four Navajo boys leaped out of a stand
of sage waving their arms and shouting. They
danced about wildly waving sticks and branches.
Big Baldy sent his mares charging away.

Ebony, Kitten, and Charlie had trailed along
after the herd. Every Navajo who saw them was
determined to catch the black stallion and the filly.
Ebony and Kitten were prizes worth more to them
than the scarred herd leader. Ebony and Kitten did
not understand what was going on, but Charlie
knew the Navajo were trying to round up the herd.

Cautious, he galloped along far behind the tiring mares. The three became thirsty and several times Charlie tried to lead them to water. When he found all of the waterholes guarded he began to look toward the distant mountains where he knew there was plenty of water which would not be guarded.

Even Big Baldy began to weaken as the chase went on. There was no rest for the horses. Every time they tried to rest, a few Navajo appeared and sent them pounding off across the desert. Night came and they had not been able to get to water. As darkness settled they found fires glowing at every watering place. Riders appeared out of the night shouting and chanting. Their horses were fresh and pushed the jaded mares hard. Big Baldy had trouble keeping the herd moving.

The next day the chase continued with the Navajo pressing hard. Toward noon four of the mares halted and refused to move on. Big Baldy had to leave them and they were quickly roped by the Indians. The ranks thinned until there was only the scarred old veteran and three of the strongest mares left.

Ebony, Kitten, and Charlie watched the final act from a high mesa. The three mares could go no farther. Seven Navajo cornered them in an arroyo and roped them, then went after the big stallion. He fought savagely when they closed in on him, but he was weak from exertion and thirst and they finally roped and hobbled him. He screamed his defiance, but he was helpless.

Charlie turned his face toward the mountains and whinnied eagerly. The three started off as a group of Navajo appeared, galloping rapidly over the hot sand. The three loners raced away with the shouting Indians on their heels. The Navajo soon gave up the chase, certain that the horses would circle back seeking water. But Charlie did not circle; he kept going toward the distant blue mountains.

Staggering with weariness, they reached the foothills and found a stream. The water was bitter with alkali but they drank, sparingly at first, then in deep drafts, sucking the bitter water in and then blowing deeply. They splashed into the water and let it soak their hoofs. Finally they moved out on the bank and cropped grass until darkness fell. Both Ebony and Charlie kept a close watch upon the ridge above them and the bend far down the stream. It was Charlie who was the really vigilant one, though Ebony was learning that he must be alert. No riders followed them and with the coming of darkness they lay down to rest.

Ebony and his two companions stayed in the foothills for several weeks, cropping the short grass and drinking bitter water. The young stallion and the filly became frisky and restless and wanted to move on, but Charlie was reluctant to return to the tall grass country where he might be rounded up and returned to captivity. Having the two young horses with him broke the bond that had existed between himself and Big Baldy's herd. Ebony and Kitten liked his companionship and that satisfied him.

A change was taking place in Ebony. As the summer wore on he became more restless. He no longer followed Charlie's leadership without question. Slowly he began to take over, selecting the meadows where they would graze, and the places they would go.

By the time the first frosts came, he was the acknowledged leader of the three. He led them up toward the mountains but not as high up as the snug valley where Big Baldy and his mares had wintered. This was not wisdom on his part; he did not remember much about the high valleys where the tall grass would cure and furnish winter food, so he stayed on the lower benches where the grass was shorter but where the snow would not be so deep. His range extended up into the aspen belt but not far into the pines and spruce. This was Bar T cattle range and when fall came there were many riders in the area looking for cattle. The three loners were sighted by a Bar T cowboy who told Tex and Major Howard about them.

It was natural for the three to be seen because they did not hide during the day. Tex took time off to catch the black stallion. He set out trailing a pack horse loaded with a bedroll and a week's supply of grub. It took him one day to locate Ebony and his pals. Watching them from cover, he recognized Kitten and Charlie at once. He decided that since the colt was friendly with a gelding, he must not be very wild. He felt certain he could rope Ebony and choke him into submission. The colt could not have already learned the fighting ways of a wild stallion.

Tex was right, Ebony had not learned many wild horse tricks and he had not developed a hatred for men; but he was wary and watchful, distrusting all large creatures except cows and steers which he had learned were placid and peaceful. The predators from the breaks above had taught him that he must not relax, that he must watch and listen. Twice he had been able to spot a cougar creeping up on Kitten, and each time he had reacted like a wild stallion—he had charged, screaming, and sent the cougar bounding away. He had even defied the old black bear and sent him on his way.

When Tex tried to ride up on him under cover of a grove, Ebony heard the mount's hoofs. He was ready when Tex charged out of the grove, swinging his rope. Ebony whinnied a warning to Kitten and Charlie before bolting for cover, but Tex's big gelding was fast and he had the advantage of moving at full speed before Ebony could get started. Tex stood up in his stirrups and swung his loop. It sailed out, snaking toward Ebony's hind quarters. Tex had planned to make a leg catch and throw the colt, and since he was an expert, his loop tightened around one hind leg close to the hock. The gelding planted his feet while Tex took a hitch around his saddle horn. The rope tightened, and Ebony was thrown on his side. He fell hard and the impact knocked the breath out of him for a few seconds, but he was up fast, lunging to his feet and rearing up.

High on a ridge Kitten and Charlie watched. Kitten whinnied wildly and stamped her feet. She wanted to run away, but she would not leave Ebony. Charlie watched and shook his head, then faded into a thicket of second-growth pines.

Tex expected Ebony to plunge again. He planned to take the starch out of the youngster by giving him a few hard falls. But Ebony was no ordinary wild stallion. He had a temper and now he was filled with rage. He hardly noticed Tex; his rage was against the big horse he thought had caused his fall. He was sure the gelding had somehow knocked him off his feet. With a scream he charged the gelding, rising on his hind feet as he closed in, baring his teeth. The gelding knew about stallions, having been attacked by the Bar T herd leader, Midnight. He went into panic at once, plunging aside and humping his back. When Tex tried to jerk him to a halt he began pitching wildly. Tex had to loosen the rope from the saddle horn and give his attention to staying in the saddle.

Ebony tried to charge again, but the free rope wrapped around his legs and tripped him. He stumbled and fell to his knees. Kicking and lashing at the rope, he whirled around several times. The noose finally loosened and he kicked free. He stood snorting and whinnying loudly and defiantly. Tex was fighting his horse to a stop a hundred yards down the slope. When he got the gelding under control he sat and watched Ebony gallop up the ridge to where Kitten stood waiting. He now knew that catching the black stallion was not a one-man job; he'd have to get Hank and at least one other rider to help him. More than ever he was impressed by the black and determined to capture him.

With Kitten, Ebony headed at once for the cover where Charlie was hidden. He had finally taken notice of Tex and decided that the combination of a man and a horse was dangerous and could not be handled like cougars or bears. He meant to put a lot of distance between himself and the horse with the rider. He started off at a lope with Kitten at his side. Charlie dropped in behind them. He, too, wanted to get away from the rider. They kept going around the mountain until Ebony felt safe and he

did not return again to the Bar T cattle range that
fall.

Winter found them in a valley close above the
desert. Tex and Hank had scoured the country
above but had not ridden that far south. The snow
that winter was light; less than a foot fell in their
valley. Deer moved down to join them and a band
of antelope drifted in. Soon two cougars and a lone
old lobo wolf arrived. One of the cougars was an
old tom and he was interested in Kitten because she
was the most likely prey. Charlie wanted to move
out. He never stayed in an area where there was
even one cougar; this valley held two. But Ebony
refused to leave the valley he had chosen, and
Charlie would not leave by himself. Ebony watched
over Kitten with such fierce vigilance that the big
tom gave up the idea of pulling down the little mare
and gave his attention to the does who had no
protection.

Late in the winter some wolves arrived, but they
soon decided to leave the horses alone. Ebony was
now a big and powerful stallion capable of killing
any wolf that attacked him or his companions. He
made it clear to the wolves that he would do just
that to any wolf that attacked.

A pair of golden eagles lived on one of the cliffs
overlooking the valley. They had an eyrie high on a

shelf which they used every spring and summer. They patrolled the air over the valley looking for rabbits, but they would also attack a fawn if it strayed into the open away from its mother. They were deadly killers, fearless and aggressive.

The winter passed without much hardship for the horses. Charlie showed his ribs, but Ebony and Kitten remained in fine shape. Grass had been easy to reach, and there was a supply of sweet cottonwood and willow along a winding stream.

With the coming of the first run-off, Ebony began to show signs of restlessness. He galloped about from one rim of the valley to the other, looking and calling. He wasn't quite sure just what was driving him, but he began to show irritation when Kitten grazed close to Charlie. Charlie sensed the change and stayed away from Kitten. Ebony was feeling the first urges of maturity. He was looking for mares—he needed more than just Kitten, he wanted a herd of his own. One spring morning he started off toward the higher country above the foothills. He nudged Kitten and even nipped her flank to make her go along with him. Charlie dropped in behind and loped along with them.

A Herd of His Own

EBONY lacked Big Baldy's wisdom. He had a lot to learn about gathering a herd. Big Baldy had known the best ranches to raid, the pastures he could safely invade and make off with range mares. Ebony headed up into the mountains where he had run with the gray stallion's herd. It was the only place he knew where there might be horses. He covered a great deal of ground, herding Kitten along, with Charlie following. Day after day they moved along ridges and across valleys. He made a great circle which brought him back to the valley where he had wintered. He found no mares and this added to his restlessness. The deer had moved up into the mountains, but the antelope had remained, flashing their white rump patches as they signaled to each other. Open sage country was the range they liked. The eagles were there too. They had repaired their eyrie and were guarding it closely.

Up on the ledge two eaglets sat in a cup on a platform of limbs and sticks. They were both well feathered and almost grown. The female was a third larger than her brother as is always the way with eagles. All through their growing-up period she had fought and beaten her brother. He was lucky to have survived with her demanding and getting most of the game brought in by their parents. But now a bond of friendship was growing between them. They sat with their big talons gripping the limbs at the edge of the cup and flapped their wings endlessly, building strength into their flight muscles. They screamed excitedly when they looked down and saw the three horses approaching the cliff.

Ebony paid no attention to the eagles until the mother dived upon him when he moved close to the base of the cliff. She was followed by her mate, who was circling above her. They would not allow any animal to get close to the cliff. The mother eagle stooped in at terrific speed and struck Ebony a smashing blow with her talons, ripping hair out of his back. The startled stallion whinnied loudly, his anger roused by the painful blow. He reared up and lashed the air with his forefeet. The father came in

but missed Ebony's back, striking instead his flying tail which was raised high. Kitten and Charlie galloped out into the meadow and halted to look back.

Ebony stubbornly stood his ground, ready to fight back at the enemy which had attacked him from the air. The female eagle rose high and rolled over, then came down in a whistling dive. This time she ripped hair out of the colt's flowing mane. Ebony found himself pitted against an enemy he could not reach. The eagles struck and were off before he could use his hoofs or teeth. He reared and screamed, smashing at his tormentors, but finally had to gallop away across the valley. Kitten and Charlie joined him and they raced a mile before halting. Having routed the intruders, the eagles spiraled high into the sky and circled on wings which remained motionless as they took advantage of the currents of air rising from the sun-warmed ground.

Up on the eyrie, the young eagles were greatly excited by the fight going on below. The female leaned far out and beat her wings furiously. Suddenly the limb under her broke and she tumbled downward. As she fell she kept on beating her wings and before she struck the ground, she was flying a wobbly course which took her out over the meadow. She landed on a sage-dotted slope close to where the three horses were standing, and tumbled end over end. She came to rest against a big clump of sage and scrambled to her feet, turning to face the horses defiantly. On the eyrie above, her brother was leaning far out, his wings working frantically as he called to her. She answered his call and he launched forward, coming down in a twisting, wavering series of spirals. He landed close to his sister and did a series of somersaults just as his sister had done. He got to his feet and sat beside her. Both thrust their heads forward and screamed at the horses. From high above the parents heard the cries and plummeted downward.

Kitten and Charlie whirled and galloped away, but Ebony stood staring at the young eagles, undecided as to what he should do about them. They might be the same enemies that had attacked him. He had them on the ground and could get at them. Whinnying loudly, he shook his head and charged toward the young eagles. They did not retreat or attempt to escape. An eagle never retreats from attack, no matter what the odds are. But before Ebony could reach the pair he was struck by the father and then by the mother eagle. Their attack made him whirl and rear up, lashing the air. Again there was nothing he could strike. The eagles were swiftly rising, getting altitude for another dive. Ebony forgot about the young eagles. The powerful talons, able to break the bones of a big animal, had bruised and raked furrows in his back. With a savage

scream, he whirled and charged away after Kitten
and Charlie.

The brush with the eagles helped make Ebony
decide that he did not like the valley. He headed
Kitten up into the hills and renewed his search for
mares. He finally sighted a small herd of horses
moving in from the desert. He was on a ridge and
they were far below, but he whinnied eagerly and
galloped down the slope with Kitten and Charlie
following him.

A gray stallion was driving the herd. Ebony did
not recognize Big Baldy; all he was interested in was
the mares. The scarred old stallion had proved to be
too savage for the Navajo to handle. He had broken
his hobbles and escaped into the desert, where he
had spent the winter foraging for mares. He had
gathered eight half-starved mares from Navajo
herds and was driving them up into the tall grass
country.

Big Baldy recognized Ebony as a rival seeking to
take over his herd. He had met and smashed many
young stallions who had sought to displace him. He
screamed loudly and charged to meet Ebony, who
accepted the challenge with savage eagerness. He
was no longer a colt unsure of himself and lacking
strong desires and urges, but had come into his own
and was filled with wild fury. He did not swerve
aside, but met Big Baldy's rush head-on, teeth slashing and hoofs smashing. They came together with

jarring force which set them both back on their hind
legs, causing their teeth and hoofs to miss their
intended targets.

Big Baldy was an experienced fighter, a veteran
of many battles. He was filled with rage and a desire
to destroy the black youngster, but he hadn't forgotten the tricks he had learned. His teeth found
Ebony's neck and sank deep as his shoulder hit the
colt, knocking him off balance. Ebony struggled to
free himself. He was filled with a rage as strong as
his opponent's, but he was fighting blindly, not trying to protect himself, simply attempting to batter
Big Baldy.

Ebony wrenched loose from the teeth that gripped
him, leaving a wound which would become his first
big battle scar, and lashed at the big gray with teeth
and hoofs. Big Baldy met the blows with smashes of
his own and his teeth found Ebony's neck again.
The angry screams of the two filled the air. The
mares stood watching for a few minutes, then started
grazing. Kitten and Charlie watched from a safe
distance. Finally Charlie loped away and stood on
a hilltop. Kitten did not move, but she was nervous,
sensing that this was an important moment for her.

Big Baldy wanted to finish the young upstart
quickly. He rushed Ebony and knocked him to his
knees, then smashed at him with his hoofs. Ebony
staggered back and reared up. He was battered and
bloody, but he had no thought of quitting. Big Baldy

was sure this was his chance to finish the youngster. He lunged with teeth bared. This time Ebony used his teeth effectively. He sank them into Big Baldy's neck and hung on. The gray screamed and shook himself loose. He dodged Ebony's hoofs, and slashed out with his own, hitting Ebony on the shoulder and ribs. The blows sent Ebony reeling backward, but he did not go down. Instead, he lunged at Big Baldy again, striking at the gray with all of the power he possessed. His heavy hoofs found their target, and when Big Baldy swerved aside he was favoring his right front leg.

Grimly the old veteran bored in again. He was met by battering hoofs and slashing teeth. Ebony was young and strong. This was his first battle with his own kind, and it aroused in him a savagery he had never before known, a desire to kill.

Big Baldy started to give ground. Seldom in his career had he ever backed away from a challenger, but now he found himself fighting a defensive game. This black horse had more power than any stallion he had ever met. He lashed and slashed with his teeth, but he retreated. Ebony was on him without let-up, tearing and battering with a fury which would not be denied. Big Baldy was beaten and knew it. All that he could hope for was to escape alive. Ducking one of Ebony's rushes, he whirled and galloped away. Ebony thundered after him, slashing at his rump. He chased Big Baldy far out into the desert before breaking off the attack. When he turned back he screamed triumphantly and galloped to where the mares were feeding.

The mares watched him come and bunched together. Kitten had moved in close to the herd and she, too, joined the bunch. Charlie was uncertain what to do. He stood on high ground and watched, then he trotted toward the mares, nickering eagerly. Ebony did not sound off or lunge at him. Charlie edged close to a wild mare. She laid back her ears and turned her tail toward him, then ignored him. Charlie felt he had been welcomed by the herd.

One young mare decided this was a good time to break away and return to her home pastures. She had feared Big Baldy, but the young black stallion did not seem surly or mean. She moved out of the herd and started to run. Ebony reacted like a veteran herd stallion. He didn't intend to lose even one mare. Whirling, he raced after the fleeing filly. He caught up with her a hundred yards from the herd and swung in at her side, shouldering her around, then nipping her hip sharply. She raced back to join the other mares.

Ebony was no longer a colt who would run a herd of mares just for the fun there was in it; now he was serious about keeping them together and protecting them. They were a sorry lot, thin and bony from lack of feed and from hard riding. They were shaggy, their winter coats had not completely shed, so there were many patches of matted hair on their backs. They had always been ridden at a gallop, so they could run and they were tough. Several of them were about to drop colts. All needed good grass, water, and rest.

Finding the grass was not difficult. There was plenty of it in the foothills, and there were clear streams. Ebony seemed to know the mares needed a chance to build up their strength. He did not force them into long runs. He and Kitten raced together, joined by Charlie, when his energy built up to a point where it demanded release.

Charlie took to the mares like a mother hen to a flock of chicks. Ebony wasn't jealous as he would have been with a strange gelding. The mares stopped kicking at Charlie and accepted him.

There was much that Ebony had to learn about protecting a herd of mares. He got no help from the mares, because they were not wild horses. He got his first lesson when a cowboy sighted the herd and started shooting. Ebony had herded his mares up into Bar T cow range, picking it because it offered the best grass he could find. One mare went down before Ebony sounded off and stampeded the herd into a deep arroyo. The cowboy tried to shoot the stallion and thus break up the herd. Ebony offered a fast-moving, ducking, dodging target and the cowboy's bullet only creased the stallion's neck. But the experience added to Ebony's knowledge of men mounted on horses. They carried guns as well as ropes. That day he held his mares in an aspen grove and watched the surrounding slopes for men on horseback. His days of careless grazing in the open during the day were over.

Ebony soon learned that he must have several escape routes along which he could stampede the herd if they were discovered. This was after another brush with cowboys which almost ended in disaster. Ebony saw two men before they were within rifle range, but he made the mistake of running mares into a box canyon. He herded them up country instead of down and was trapped.

With the riders hot on the trail, Ebony was forced to drive his mares up along a narrow ledge, the only trail out of the box canyon. It was Charlie who found the trail leading upward. He was in a hurry to get away from the mounted men. Kitten and two mares followed him up along the ledge. Ebony screamed and sent the others up after Charlie. The mares had learned that he could use his teeth when he was angry. They scrambled upward, plunging and leaping over projecting rocks. Kitten shouldered past the cautious Charlie and leaped upward like a big horn sheep.

The cowboys rounded a bend and pulled up. Ebony was still urging two mares heavy with colt up the ledge; the other mares and Charlie had vanished over the rim.

"Too far for a shot," one of the men said.

"Be a shame to shoot that big black," the other answered. "I'd sure like to own him."

His companion laughed. "He'd shake the daylights out of you if you ever got on his back."

"Yeah. Have to kill him to tame him, I guess," the cowboy agreed.

After that encounter Ebony was as careful as Big Baldy had ever been. He knew now what to expect if his herd was sighted by riders. He explored the range and found the ravines and canyons he could use to elude pursuit. And the mares began to learn wild ways; they were off in a flash the moment he sounded the alarm. They were filling out too, gaining weight and strength. They had shed their matted winter coats and were sleek. Their Navajo owners would not have recognized them.

The two mares dropped their foals, one a filly, the other a tough little colt with a white star in his face and a blocky head like his father, Big Baldy. Ebony treated them as though they were his own offspring; he was ready to smash a wolf, coyote, or cougar who sought to dine on horsemeat.

After sighting other range riders, Ebony drove his herd into the high country where Big Baldy had kept his mares most of the time. This was familiar country to him, but he had to explore it. When he had ranged there before he had paid little attention to canyons and benches with heavy cover close to them.

The two cowboys who had chased the herd were Bar T boys. They reported sighting the herd and gave a glowing description of the black stallion with them. Major Howard had received word that Big Baldy had escaped from the Navajo, and the major was certain the gray stallion would return with a harem. He had given orders to his men to shoot any wild horse on sight, especially the gray stallion. The fact that the stallion the men described was a fine horse did not matter; he had lost interest in the idea that the black was a son of Midnight and Black Lady. He had declared war on wild horses. Four of his fine recaptured mares seemed certain to present him with foals fathered by Big Baldy. He wouldn't listen to any talk from Tex.

Tex was convinced that the young black stallion was the son of Midnight. He was also sure he knew why the herd was led by the black: Ebony had challenged Big Baldy and won. The black stallion was certainly the property of Major Howard even though he did not carry the Bar T brand, and although the major didn't want him, Tex did. At any rate he had to see the black again. He remembered the beauty of the young horse he had tried to rope. He spoke to Hank about it.

"Think I'll take a couple of days off and poke

around up in the breaks above the horse pasture," he said. They were sitting in the shade of a cotton-wood tree eating their lunch.

Hank took a bite out of his sandwich before he answered. "Could be you'll need a bit of help if you dab a rope on that black; he's grown up now."

Tex nodded. "Yeah," he agreed.

They both knew it was settled. Hank would go with Tex. He was as eager to see the black stallion and catch him as Tex was.

It was natural for Tex and Hank to ride the upper range; it was part of their job. Major Howard gave Tex a free hand in running the Bar T crew. The cattle had all been pushed up into high country and the mares were with Midnight in the horse pasture. Before he left, Tex had a word with the men. They could follow the major's orders to shoot wild mares, but they were to lay off the black stallion until he gave the word. The major need not know that Tex had given the stallion a stay of execution. The men understood and would do as Tex ordered. Few among them liked the idea of shooting any kind of a horse, wild or not.

Tex and Hank trailed along a light pack outfit. When they reached the horse pasture, they checked the Bar T mares and found them all present, with Midnight in charge. The big black stallion sounded an angry warning when he scented the geldings Tex and Hank were riding. He was tame, but not completely domesticated. The major had never tried to make a barnyard stallion out of him. He had a theory that the wild strain would add mettle and spirit to the fillies and colts Midnight fathered.

Hank squinted at the big fellow and shook his head. "That young black just can't match him," he said.

"Let's just hope that they never get together to decide," Tex said thoughtfully. He was aware that the young stallion might challenge Midnight. It seemed certain that he had met and beaten Big Baldy, a tough old fighter. If they met, the result could be disaster. If anything happened to ruin Midnight, the major would really go on the warpath.

They rode on up country keeping a careful watch on benches, ridges, and valleys, moving slowly and keeping to cover. They saw no horses except three stray Lazy Y mares. Sighting the mares convinced Tex that Ebony was not on that part of the range; if he had been anywhere near, he would have added the mares to his herd. So the two cowboys headed on up into the broken country above the cow range.

Late in the afternoon of the second day, they came to a beaver pond. On its upper bank, they found horse tracks. Tex dismounted and studied the tracks. He decided there were eight or nine mares with the stallion. One set of tracks puzzled him. They were big and deep. He had a hunch they were not the tracks of a mare, but he couldn't accept them as anything else, not with Ebony's deep prints close to them. He had completely forgotten that there had been a big gelding with the colt when he last saw him. But his greatest interest was in the tracks of the black stallion. They indicated that he had added a lot of weight. The prints showed not a trace of blemish or lameness in the horse that had made them.

He looked up at Hank and grinned. "We're getting mighty close," he said.

"Not more than a day old," Hank answered. He had been studying the seepage in one of the tracks.

Tex squinted up at the sun. "We might spot them before dark."

"If he's grown up, we won't see any mares before dark." Hank pushed back his hat and looked up the slope the tracks took as they left the pond.

They rode up into a stand of spruce and pine, moving slowly and stopping often. When they reached the top of the ridge, they pulled up and studied the country around them. The parks were very small with dense cover. A steep-walled ravine cut its way down past a wooded slope. Tex decided that the wooded slope above the ravine would be ideal cover for a small herd of horses. When he pointed it out, Hank nodded his head. They circled around and approached the wooded area from above.

Ebony was restless. He had had a brush with old

Clubfoot that morning. The surly old fellow was again at war with the brothers who were now fully grown. They didn't run together any more, but they still liked the king bear's domain. It was rich in roots and berries. They refused to run out of the rough country. The king had been chasing them all morning and had worked himself into a raging mood. He had stumbled upon the mares and had scattered them before Ebony could charge in and send the big bear galloping out of the grove.

Ebony had spent some time rounding up his mares and quieting them down. On this occasion, Charlie hadn't been any help, he had panicked worse than the mares and made a lot of noise charging through the underbrush. Ebony prowled about, keeping on the move. The timber was so heavy it was not easy to spot even a big black bear.

A breeze was blowing down from above the timber line. Ebony tested it at intervals. His sense of smell and his sight were very sharp, and his hearing was that of a wild creature. He caught the scent of the approaching geldings when they were still some distance above him. Listening, he heard a twig snap. He stood peering up through the timber, trying to discover the source of the sound. Presently he saw Tex, who was riding ahead of Hank, and then he saw Hank's battered hat moving above a stand of choke-cherry. The riders were visible for only a brief moment, but that was enough time to make Ebony whirl and sound off as he dashed down through the timber.

His scream instantly alerted the mares. They closed ranks and fled toward the rim of the ravine with Ebony lashing at their swaying rumps. The two colts fled at their mothers' sides, pressing close to them. Charlie was out in front because he was at the lower edge of the grove. He preferred to bring up the rear where he could pick his way carefully down the steep embankment, but he had no choice. He had to plunge down the steep wall or be trampled by the stampeding mares.

Tex and Hank knew instantly that they had flushed the herd. They galloped down through the timber and pulled up on the rim of the ravine, arriving in time to watch Ebony send his herd down the abrupt drop off. Tex caught his breath as he watched the magnificent stallion in action.

"He's a mite bigger and heavier than Midnight," Hank observed.

"Best piece of horseflesh I ever set eyes on," Tex said. "Have to get the major up here to have a look at him." Tex was sure that if the major saw the black stallion, nothing would keep him from capturing the horse. It would be a sure way to save the big fellow, but it had to be done at once. He could not risk having father and son meet. The resulting battle would be sure to cripple one or both.

"He'll carry the Bar T brand if the major ever sets eyes on him," Hank agreed.

Meat Hunters

EBONY decided the wooded slopes on top of the mountain offered no secure refuge from riders; men could slip up on the herd even if it was hidden in a grove of trees. After leaving the ravine, he headed his mares around the mountain and down toward the desert in a western direction. He chose to go west because he remembered that the Navajo roamed the desert to the south. He had no knowledge of the desert beyond the brief time he had spent there while following Big Baldy's herd. And he was heading into territory he knew nothing about.

The herd set an easy pace across the sage-covered foothills. Ebony could check the entire sweep of country from the top of a hill or from a rimrock.

He could see any riders who might be approaching, miles before they got near the mares. The air was clear, making it possible to see moving objects at a great distance. Mountains fifty miles away looked no more than an hour's traveling distance away from the foothills of the Crazy Kill range.

The desert below was a many-colored expanse of rims and spires and sand dunes. Great shafts of red-and-yellow sandstone stood alone on the desert floor, isolated where the formations around them had eroded away. They looked like giant goblins crouching silently amid arroyos and twisting, dry canyons. Far to the east a hundred miles away, ship rock, a towering pinnacle, lifted its spires like a ship under full sail. The heat waves flowing over the expanses of sand gave it movement.

The beauty of the desert went unnoticed by Ebony and his mares. They moved along, cropping the scanty bunch grass, occasionally nibbling at a bunch of salt sage. The hot sun beat down on them, and their backs were soon streaked with dust collected by the sweat from their bodies. A hot wind stirred up eddies of fine sand and carried the smell of sage with it.

They came to a small stream which flowed west into the desert and followed it. Ebony had his eyes on a distant range of mountains. He had no way of knowing that they were a hundred miles away; their

blue ramparts looked no more than ten miles distant. As the herd moved along, the stream became
shallower and narrower. The sand absorbed much

of it, and the hot sun evaporated a great deal.
Finally the stream disappeared entirely and the herd
was following a dry wash, its bed a smooth expanse
of dry sand. The hoofs of the horses sank into the

sand, making walking hard work. The herd plodded along with the mares looking back at the lush mountain they had left.

Charlie halted often and stood looking back. He knew going on was foolish and wanted to turn back, but he didn't want to go alone. He was torn between his fear of the desert ahead and his fear of being alone. He finally dropped in behind Ebony and plodded along.

Toward evening of the second day in the desert, the mares were very thirsty. There was no hint of water on the hot wind which blew into their faces. Soon the wind grew stronger and presently it had reached the force of a gale. It gathered up the fine sand and filled the air with it until the horses seemed to move amid a yellow glow. The mares turned their backs to the sandstorm and lowered their heads. Ebony urged them on, changing his course to a northerly direction. He was prepared to return to the foothills if he could find water. His herd could not last another day on the desert without a drink.

The mares plodded on through the night. In the early hours of the morning the storm blew itself out, and the sun shone on a changed world. The wind had reshaped the face of the desert, shifting big dunes, uncovering beds of rocks, filling arroyos. Only the pillars and spires remained the same.

A lone cottonwood tree lifted its branches above a flat mesa. Ebony headed his herd toward it. Instinct told him that where a cottonwood grew, there might be water. As they neared the tree, the mares caught the smell of water and burst into a gallop. The two colts wobbled along at their mothers' sides. They had suffered more than the grown horses. Charlie whinnied eagerly as he pounded along far ahead of the mares.

Close to the cottonwood they found a willow-bordered pond fed by a spring, shaded by a big tree. The mares crowded down the bank and thrust their muzzles into the water. Ebony was so thirsty he shouldered in among the mares and drank.

There was enough grass growing around the oasis to feed the herd for a couple of days. The mares were loath to leave the grass and the water. Ebony did not urge them, but he had decided that when they did move, it would be back to the Crazy Kill Mountains. He had had enough of the desert.

But even in this isolated place there was danger. A crew of meat hunters had the spring spotted. They had mapped out the whole area so they could check the waterholes daily, knowing that wild horses of the desert had to come to these watering places.

Clint Hoff, one of the meat hunters, spotted Ebony and his herd through field glasses. He rode back to camp to report to his boss, Mike Peal.

"Nine mares, two colts, a big stallion, and a gelding out at Cottonwood Spring," he reported.

Mike Peal scowled. He hadn't made a big catch all spring. This was a small herd. Mike was a big man with a long beaklike nose that was constantly peeling from sunburn. He knew nothing about horses except that he could sell them to a dog-food processing plant. This herd would bring a little over four hundred dollars.

"We'll go get them along toward evening," he said gruffly.

Mike's operation was a simple but deadly one. He had two four-wheel-drive trucks geared for speed. His crew consisted of six men beside himself. Each truck was manned by a driver and two rope men. The driver's job was to overtake fleeing horses so the rope hands could lasso them. Each rope had a heavy truck tire tied to it. Once a horse was roped, the tire was tossed out of the truck. The drag of the tire would soon choke the horse into a helpless condition and it was then loaded into the big truck. Few wild horses ever escaped once Mike Peal sighted them. Mike's strategy was, first, to rope the leader if there was a stallion with the herd. After he had the stallion the mares were easy to catch. No horse could outrun his big trucks. The horses had to be delivered alive to the plant or to a siding on a railroad. If they were choked to death, the meat would spoil before it could be delivered.

Mike Peal's methods were frowned upon by cattlemen, even though they themselves destroyed wild horses. Horse lovers hated him, but there was nothing they could do about it. The territory he picked was in the public domain. Getting Congress to pass a law protecting wild horses was a difficult thing to do. Mike had nothing to fear from state laws, and he did not mind the contempt the natives had for him.

Ebony moved restlessly around his herd. The mares were resting close to the spring, many of them lying down. They had fed well and had recovered somewhat from the ordeal in the desert. Charlie grazed apart from the herd. He seemed to know that he should eat as much as he could to prepare for another long trip across the hot sand. The coolness of night had not yet settled. When it did, Ebony would move his herd, driving them back to the mountains.

The young stallion stood on a dune watching the eroded country around him. His first warning of danger came when he heard the sound of truck motors. He saw no trucks; the sound came from the direction of a deep arroyo. Then suddenly there were two big trucks, appearing like monsters, out of nowhere. Their huge tires rolled over the sand without sinking in. Once on level ground, they headed for the spring with motors roaring. These surplus army trucks needed no roads; nor did they need smooth ground.

Ebony screamed a warning. The mares who were lying down leaped to their feet. The herd crowded together and charged away into the desert with Ebony lashing at the slower mares. Charlie showed the least concern of all. He knew about trucks; no truck had ever harmed or bothered him. He stood and watched for a few moments before galloping after the herd.

Mike Peal was in the lead truck. He pointed toward Ebony, and the driver beside him nodded as he pushed the gas pedal to the floor boards. Neither man took time to admire the big stallion. Mike was pleased only because the black was big and in fine condition. He would bring a bonus.

Even without the mares to slow him down, Ebony could not have outrun the truck. He lashed at the mares and screamed, but the roaring demon pursuing him rapidly caught up and closed in on him. The driver pulled alongside the charging stallion, and one of the rope hands swung his loop. The man was not expert, but he was so close he could not miss. The loop dropped over Ebony's head and the third man in the truck heaved a heavy tire over the side. The truck swerved and plowed away after one of the mares.

The rope sank into Ebony's neck as it tightened, and the big tire bounced as his weight put pressure on it. Lunging and kicking, Ebony dragged the heavy tire. He strained against the rope, but it only sank onto his neck more, shutting off his air with a choking pressure. He went on plunging until the lack of air made him stagger. Finally he went down, plowing a furrow in the sand, his big hoofs beating helplessly.

The mares, with the trucks pursuing them, had scattered. Charlie was roped at once, and one by one the mares went down. The hunters did not have to worry about the horses getting away once they were roped.

Ebony shook his head and raised it. The choking rope had loosened enough to allow him to breathe. As soon as he recovered his breath he lunged to his feet. Around him the desert sand was dotted with helpless horses, some down, others still fighting the rope around their necks. He plunged away and again the drag on the rope choked him and he fell hard. This time consciousness left him and he lay quivering and heaving.

The hunters began the work of loading the horses, being careful to see to it that none died. All they wanted was enough life left in the mares so that they could be loaded. Ramps were dropped at the backs of the trucks and the weakened animals pushed up into the trucks.

Mike left Ebony to the last. He wanted the black stallion to have only enough life left in him to allow him to stand and be shoved into a truck. Ebony had fought the rope and the tire a half dozen times and when a truck pulled up beside him, he was so weak he could barely remain on his feet. As the ramp dropped before him he made one last lunge which carried him up into the truck. Mike Peal laughed loudly; the fool horse hadn't even needed a push. The tailgate was slammed into place and latched. Mike waved a signal to the other truck. The hunt was over; all the grown horses had been caught. Only the two young colts remained; they were not worth loading. They whinnied wildly and circled about on the desert.

Ebony found himself wedged in between Kitten and Charlie. Mike had noticed the brands but figured he could get away with selling two branded horses. The meat buyer never asked questions. Horsemeat was too much in demand for them to be careful. Mike always dealt with that type of buyer.

The truck ground along, only halting long enough at the hunters' camp to load their bedrolls and other equipment on top of the truck cabs. Then they headed for a pass north of the Crazy Kill Mountains.

Ebony recovered quickly. He ripped at the tailgate of the truck with his teeth. There wasn't room enough for him to use his hoofs to batter down the gate; he was wedged in too tightly.

When the trucks reached the pass, Mike Peal decided to stop and cook supper. The men were tired and needed food. He felt pleased enough with the catch to bring out a bottle of whisky and pass it around. Before the meal was cooked the men were laughing and talking drunkenly. Mike didn't mind. They would sober up after they had had some food.

No thought was given to watering the horses even though a cold stream flowed past the campsite. The horses coughed to clear the dust from their lungs. They stamped their feet and whinnied. Many of the mares were in bad shape. One of them in Ebony's truck sank down against the forward wall of the truck. She kicked feebly, then lay still. Her colt had been left with the filly to die on the desert. The will to protect him had given her extra courage in fighting the choking rope, and she had suffered more than the others. Now she was through fighting.

With the mare down, there was more room. Ebony pressed Kitten and Charlie back until he had room to rear up and smash at the tailgate. He made a lot of noise as he battered away, screaming savagely with every blow. At the fire Clint Hoff laughed loudly as he took a pull out of the second bottle Mike had opened.

"Listen to that old boy sound off," he shouted.

Everyone laughed loudly, but no one got up to see what was going on. In the truck, Ebony was making progress; the gate was splintering. One board flew off and then another. Ebony's power gave his hoofs the impact of two sledge hammers. Finally the last section of the gate broke loose and fell away. Instantly Ebony leaped out of the truck, followed by Kitten and Charlie. Ebony did not wait for the other two live mares in the truck. He sent Kitten galloping toward a dark mass of timber. Before entering the woods he whirled and halted long enough to send a wild scream ringing down toward the camp.

Ebony's cry was the first warning Mike Peal had that some of the horses had escaped. He ran toward the truck and arrived in time to see two mares make leaps to freedom. He bellowed loudly and his men came running. One of them had caught up a rifle and started blasting away at the fleeing horses. Mike knocked the gun aside.

"They're no good dead," he snarled. "They'll go back to the desert and we'll get them later."

There was nothing the hunters could do about

recapturing the horses. The country was too rough, and there was too much timber to use the truck. Mike had to be satisfied with the mares he still had. They would not bring enough to pay for the hunt, but they would be better than nothing.

Ebony soon gathered up the two Navajo mares and started his little herd moving. He headed them toward the Crazy Kill Mountains and kept them going through the starlit night. The only halt was at a stream where they drank deeply. His rage at the meat hunters had cooled. Black hatred for men had taken its place. There seemed to be no spot where a wild horse could be safe from this two-legged enemy.

A New Home

THE YOUNG STALLION was sure of one thing—he wanted a range far from the haunts of man if that was possible. But before he sought such a place he had to gather a few more mares. He had only Kitten and the two Navajo mares. The only place he knew where there were mares was the high range above the ranches or the ranches themselves. So he headed his little herd down off the divide toward the Crazy Kill country he knew.

Conditions were ideal. There was a moon at night. By day the horses stayed in deep cover. Kitten had become a wild horse in every way. No longer did she graze in the open during the daytime. Charlie, too, had become as wary as any wild mare.

Ebony found his first mares on the Lazy Y range. There were four mares and three geldings in the herd. They had wandered into high country to escape from heel flies and to get away from over-grazed meadows. The young stallion drove the geldings down country, chasing them more than a mile. Then he rounded up the four mares and quickly taught them to obey his commands, especially the rule about keeping to cover during the day.

He added five more mares which he took from a scrub stallion who had picked them up one at a time. The scrub stallion fled after a brief clash with Ebony. Four of the mares were unbranded; the other was a Bar T fence buster who was the despair of Tex and his men. She would have made a good mate for Big Baldy because she was a jumper. Major Howard had made up his mind to sell her when they again caught her.

Ebony now had ten fine mares, plus the two shaggy little Navajo ponies. These were no longer lean and underfed, but they would never be able to stay with the herd in a real stampede. And they never could get used to the forest and the rugged breaks. Ebony lost them a few days after he captured the five mares.

It was late in the afternoon and Ebony was holding his herd in a stand of lodge-pole pines on the rim of a deep canyon. He was on guard at a spot from which he could watch the ridge leading up to the hideout as well as the trail leading down, when he sighted two riders coming up the trail, heading straight toward the pine cover. They were a mile away, but he did not wait. He sent his mares charging through the timber. The trees grew so close together that the mares had to dodge and swerve in and out. The two ponies did very well while they were in the timber; they were nimble and could slip through the openings the bigger mares had to go around. But when the herd plunged down to the floor of the canyon and raced up its dry bed they were left behind.

In the dust raised by flying hoofs Ebony did not miss them. When the ponies finally slowed down, they climbed out of the canyon and stood looking down over the slopes and ridges. Far below lay the desert, stretching to a distant horizon. The older pony started off, heading down country. The other pony followed. They would steadily bear south, drawn by the lure of the dry mesas and arroyos where they had been born and had grown up.

When Ebony missed the ponies he searched for them briefly before moving on into higher country. After two days of travel the herd came to a wild valley encircled by towering peaks. The floor of the valley was strewn with boulders scattered about as though two armies of giants had staged a battle there, hurling huge boulders at each other. Brush and tall grass grew between the rocks, and there was a stream of clear cold water flowing through the valley. The slopes on every side were heavily wooded.

Ebony explored the valley carefully and found two routes which could serve as exits, a narrow canyon and an elk trail which led out over a low pass. This was a fine place for a wild-horse herd. Foals would soon be adding to the herd. Ebony settled down, watching for predators and for the sight of mounted men. No man could enter the valley except by the pass or up the canyon, and he could spot them hours before they could get close enough to see the herd.

Word of a beautiful black stallion and a herd of mares came to Tex from an elk hunter who packed into the valley, hunting. Tex got permission from Major Howard to take a week off, and he and Hank packed into the valley. They used every wild-horse trick they knew. Looking the valley over from the pass, Tex decided that it would cost more than the major would ever spend to trap the stallion and his mares in that wild gorge. He and Hank sat their horses in a dense willow thicket close to a spring.

"We can sneak down there and clean them out," Hank said.

Tex shook his head. "I don't go for just plain

killing of horses." He smiled. "But I sure want to see that ebony stallion."

They dismounted and made the long climb down into the valley. It took them four hours of sneaking and crawling to locate the grove where Ebony was holding his herd. They first spotted Charlie standing under a pine tree; then one by one they sighted the mares. Hank nudged Tex.

He's got the fence buster," he whispered.

Tex nodded. His eyes were on a little knoll where he had a feeling the black stallion would appear. After fifteen minutes of waiting, Ebony did appear on the knoll, his head lifted, ears forward, mane and tail flowing in the stiff breeze. Both men caught their breaths at the sight of the big horse. Tex sighed.

"Want to try for him?" Hank whispered. "I might be able to crease him with a bullet and knock him out."

"No," Tex said. "I'll come back next summer and see if he has sired a colt with his class." Tex turned and started to crawl away. Hank followed. They were careful not to expose themselves.

"If we'd shown ourselves, he'd have run his herd out of that valley," Tex added when they reached their horses. "I sort of like the idea of his having found such a good spot . . . sort of a horse heaven."